I0684546

SAINT SMITH

AND OTHER STORIES

RICHARD SELTZER

Saint Smith excerpted from Sandcastles Copyright © 1987, 1989, 1991 by Richard Seltzer
The Barracks Copyright © 1989, 1990 by Richard Seltzer
The Choice Copyright © 2009 by Richard Seltzer
The Gentle Inquisitor Copyright © 1977 by Richard Seltzer, first published in **Aspect** #68
The Mirror Copyright © 1991 by Richard Seltzer

Published by
B&R Samizdat Express
33 Gould St.
West Roxbury, MA 02132
http://samizdat.stores.yahoo.net/
http://www.samizdat.com

ISBN: 1455400866
ISBN-13: 9781455400867

Printed in the United States of America, January 2011

First Edition

Also by Richard Seltzer:
Echoes from the Attic, a contemporary novel (with Ethel Kaiden)
The Name of Hero, an historical novel
The Lizard of Oz, a satiric fantasy
Now and Then and Other Tales from Ome, children's stories
The AltaVista Search Revolution
Web Business Bootcamp

Thanks to Rex Sexton for many years of encouragement and advice; and to my wife Barbara for her infinite patience and brilliant insights; and in memory of my mother, Helen Isabella Estes Seltzer, from whom I inherited and learned the need to write.

CONTENTS

SAINT SMITH

CHAPTER ONE
CONTAGIOUS DREAMS

July 1966, Silver Spring, Maryland

The rest of the family was gathered in the living room playing instruments or singing songs, for the grandparents' sixtieth anniversary. Frank escaped upstairs, unnoticed in the dense crowd of relatives. He heard a noise nearby and found Irene, his uncle Charlie's wife, stretched out on her back on the bed in the guest room. With her dress awry, the upper part of one thigh was exposed. Frank stopped and stared. Then she sat up, looked at him, and smiled.

"Was denkst du?" she asked. She sometimes let him practice German with her, for the beginner's course he was taking in college. When he didn't answer right away, she asked again in English, "What are you thinking?"

Frank asked, rather than answered, "How did you get your name? Irene isn't a German name, is it?"

"That name I chose," she said. "Helga my parents called me. Ich heisse Helga, Helga Heinz."

"Then Helga's your real name," he concluded.

"No, my real name is Irene. Helga they called me."

"And what does Irene mean?"

"Peace. And before Irene, Iris my name was."

"Iris?"

"The rainbow — messenger of the gods. A bold name, nicht wahr?"

"Why change your name twice? Were you trying to hide something?" he asked.

"When you change, your name should change. Your name should harmony with you have."

"What?"

"The presence of God have you felt?" she asked, gesturing for him to sit beside her on the bed.

From downstairs, the volume of the music increased as the family reached the refrain of "A Mighty Fortress Is Our God."

The guest room was filled with conflicting shadows from the light in the hall and from the moon outside the window. There were two single beds in the room. Frank's father and his Uncle Fred had slept there as boys. Later, the room had been his uncle Charlie's. Pennants from the University of Maryland, where Charlie had been accepted and planned to go, still adorned the walls.

Charlie's high school wrestling trophies still filled a bookcase in the corner. Granny had interspersed glass elephants and giraffes among the trophies and on the bureaus and windowsills. She had hung a brass crucifix between the windows. Over one bed, the one that had been Charlie's and that Irene and Frank were on now, hung a framed reproduction of a painting with a determined-looking young man, very much like Charlie, holding the steering wheel of a ship and looking up and ahead, while Christ stood behind him with a hand on his shoulder.

"This crazy woman, you think. Religious nut, nicht wahr? But me back in Heidelburg, that you should see. Iris – the messenger – I was. Now Irene – peace – my name is."

She put her hand on his shoulder.

Frank looked up at the painting of Christ and the ship's pilot and felt a twinge of guilt. Irene was the most sensuous woman he had ever met. He was hoping for the miracle of a caress. Instead, she spoke of God.

"Have you ever God beside you felt? God Himself, living and breathing?"

He stared at her, lost in her deep blue eyes.

"Imagine that Christ returned, and you his return made happen," she said. "Or imagine each of us Christ is. A spark within us from God comes. And, sometimes, that spark can flare and brightly burn.

"I'm silly think you. Sehr gut. Perhaps my words no truth hold. What could this crazy lady know?

"I will you a story tell. The story of Der Heilige Schmidt. Heinrich Schmidt his parents him called. Heilige Schmidt we came to call him. Hank Smith, Saint Smith would you call him.

"All Sturm und Drang, all struggle and push, was I, like Charlie now. I would my mark on the world make. Very proud was I of my cleverness.

"I drama and literature studied, at Heidelberg. One day I great literature would write. Already, to me the world a stage was. My living, what I did and what I said would a masterpiece make."

"Performance art?" Frank suggested.

"What you say — yes. Only not so big a deal. At the beer keller, my friends and I tales and jokes made — not just with words, with what we did."

"Practical jokes?".

"Yes, that we did. Heinrich sometimes with us joked, but shy he was, quiet. We mocked; we laughed; we tricked."

"He was the butt of your jokes?"

"Yes, perfect was he as victim — everything he believed.

"He was gullible."

"'Ghost bags' we made."

"What are those?" Frank asked.

"Hot-air balloons, yourself you make. You this for fun at college do, nicht wahr?"

"No," he admitted.

"Ach! This must you learn. First, a cross with two pieces of wire you make. Little candles, birthday candles where the wires cross you melt. Plastic bag for clothes you take."

"Dry cleaners' bag?"

"Yes, and bag to wires you tape, with bag wide open."

"Okay. So why bother? What can you do with it?"

"At night, on roof you go, tall roof. The candles you light, the bag you hold. The bag with hot air fills. Let go. Let fly. For miles will it go. Bag with smoke filled, light bright and ghostlike shines.

"This we did, from the roof of Heinrich's building. Ten bags, one after the other. One of us with him in his room was. Heinrich the ghost bags saw — lights through the city flying. Heinrich through the halls ran, 'Fliegende geiste!' he shouted."

"You mean flying saucers?"

"Yes. A week he classes missed."

"Okay. I get it. He was embarrassed. He couldn't show his face."

"As you say. Then telephone, we the telephone trick did."

"What trick?:

"You lessons on pranks need? So simple – telephone and ball point pen. Telephone a dial has, and a receiver. When down the receiver goes, down the buttons go; and the call ends. Pen a metal clip has, for pocket. And clip round part has, like ring. From two pens the ring take. Rings on buttons put, so receiver rests; buttons don't down go; call ends not.

"Like this, I Heinrich's phone fixed. Receiver down but phone on. I with the dial played – like fooling. I my own number dialed. When to my room I went phone still rang. When I receiver picked up, everything from Heinrich's room I heard.

"Like a bug?"

"Yes, homemade bug. No cost, just fun. Friends in my room listened. Heinrich in his room lines from play practiced. We at him laughed. He laughs heard, but where the noise came from, he knew not. He shouted. We louder laughed. He here and there ran, everywhere looked – where this sound? We louder laughed.

"He must have been freaking out."

"Freaking, yes. That word. Very scared. Ran very fast, very far. Room geistlich."

"Haunted."

"Yes. Good laugh."

"Okay. So you pulled some practical jokes on him. What's the big deal? "

"The big deal next came. A play I wrote – 'All God's Children.' Satan God tells, 'Why to Earth you go? Why to Earth you your Son send? Why with man games play? All people your children are, nicht wahr? One man, any man, wake up. To one man truth make known – the truth that he God is.'

5

"In my play, God said, 'Sehr gut. Miracles from inside make, not outside. Miracles not from God; from man by the free will of man. I will one awaken, one to be to all the rest a guide. One of my children among them god-like to be.'

"In my play, God a carpenter chose. And to waken him, no angels, no burning bush came. His brothers and friends a joke played.

"Imagine Jesus at age twelve. To his parents, obedient and trustworthy was he – a fine young man. He with his father worked; he with his mother helped. To his brothers proud and pompous was he. 'Little God' they him called.

"One night, when he slept, his brother James near his face a torch waved, then ran. Outside the window, others shouted, 'I am the Light!' He did not wake. Nothing. The next night, again they tried, again he slept. And a third night, and again he slept.

"Then the morning after the third try, Jesus a new person appeared – selfless, humble, kind. To everyone he listened, for everyone he cared. His look and his words everyone comforted and inspired. 'A light unto the world' he became.

"Proud was I of this idea. But my friends mocked. Real people like this do not act. To prove my point, I myself tried. There and then, a modern version of that same joke, with Heinrich as victim I played.

"A tape recorder and camera flash I near his bed placed, with timer. In the middle of the night, the bulb would flash and the recorder would boom, "I am the light!"

"What would he think? How would he act? At least down the hall would he run and scream. More flying saucers, more laughs for us. Wild tales would he tell.

"But nothing. He just slept. So again I tried, and yet again, as in the play. Still nothing. . I stopped. Mein Gott, was I foolish.

"Then a week later, Heinrich changed. He with warmth, concern, and tenderness glowed. His deep blue eyes they compelled. His voice, his words they resounded. Even strangers everywhere him followed. With these followers, he the streets roamed, night and day. Good will and joy he spread. The poor and homeless help he gave. No preaching, just doing. Such confidence. Such strength of will.

"Me and my friends – we who had nothing believed – we, too, his followers became. Der Heilige Heinrich, Der Heilige Schmidt, Saint Smith we called him. And my friends named me 'Iris', crediting me, my play, my joke for this miracle. A 'messenger of the gods' was I for this new cult.

"Only Heinrich didn't know. No one about my trick had told him. No idea had he a joke this change had made. I what I had done must confess.

"In public him I told, so friends and followers would hear. Before him I knelt like to a God, and begged forgiveness.

"His eyes blank and cold became. Who was this? Not Der Heilige Schmidt and not the old Heinrich. I screamed. Him I grabbed. Him I hugged. Him I shook. Gone. The magic, the godliness gone.

"Then knew I that I had loved him. As God-in-man I had loved him. That heilige man had I loved.

"The cult ended. The followers they blamed me. 'Fraulein Judas' they me called.

"With him I stayed. With my body I him loved. No soul. No magic. Flesh rubbed flesh.

"I became pregnant. I an abortion had. I Heinrich left. I the university left. Irene I called myself. Peace I needed."

As she paused – Frank became aware of the music from downstairs, the chorus of "Gloria In Excelsis Deo." His muscles were

7

stiff. He hadn't moved during her narration. His right leg had gone asleep, but he didn't dare shake it. He didn't want to disturb her concentration. He wanted her to continue.

"You at my eyes stare," she noted, "not in them, but at them. Yes. They are blue, like Heinrich's, but not heilige. When he God was, when god-in-him was, his eyes you out of yourself drew. I this story poorly tell; even in German poorly. Forgive my awkward words. If once you see, no need for words. If not, words nothing do.

"Sometimes Charlie that look has. When I him in Munich first met, he that look had. He, a GI with a camera, on a street in Munich stopped me. In broken German said he, my 'face' he needed, as a model. He would me pay. Well knew I that not my face he wanted. He me followed, pictures taking. At the corner, I stopped, turned, and smiled. 'Okay,' said I in English, 'let's about your pictures talk.'

"We to a beer keller went. The story of Der Heilige Schmidt I him told, not like a story I had lived, but like a story I had written. His eyes then, they looked deep like Heinrich's. On and on we talked about the Saint Smith story, about making a movie based on that. A masterpiece it could be, said he. First must he master his craft. .

"At our wedding, too, his eyes that deep look had. And sometimes too, his eyes even now that way flash even, when me he wants and only me."

"Frankie!" his mother bellowed from downstairs. With a start, Frank reawakened to the world in which his parents treated him as if he were still a little kid. He hated being called Frankie. "Frankie!" she bellowed again.

"Yes, Mom?" he called back automatically.

"Get down here this instant. Are you deaf? It's time to go home."

With his right leg still painfully asleep, he stumbled and hobbled to the door. Irene didn't notice. She kept looking in the same direction and with the same expression. He didn't want to disturb her, and besides, he had to hurry. But he wondered if she continued to talk, even after he left.

CHAPTER TWO
MANSIONS AND CASTLES

August 1940, Silver Spring, Maryland

"Sarah, you did write the boys, didn't you?"

"Yes, Hank. Of course." Sarah poured him a cup of coffee. The kitchen seemed larger than before. She had to stretch to reach the breakfast dishes in the cabinet and to put them in their proper places at the table. "You know I write every day."

Hank gulped his coffee. "Wyoming isn't on the other side of the world. How long could it take for a letter to get there? They should have started home when Sue first turned sick." His voice dropped. "Now she's been dead a week... Where in God's creation are they?"

Sarah stopped. She didn't need to put a plate at Sue's place. "Yes. Of course. In God's creation."

Hank looked up at his wife in surprise – a delayed reaction to the bitter taste of unsweetened coffee. At that moment he realized her voice had changed. It was like the voice of some older relative of hers – familiar, but strange.

He looked at her more closely as she returned the extra plate to the cabinet, then adjusted her own plate, fork and spoon. A few streaks of gray in her black hair framed her face and gave it definition. If nature hadn't provided those streaks, a hairstylist might have. Hers wasn't the fragile beauty of youth that changed with a shift of mood, or the beauty of middle age that changed with fashions. She knew who she was and was pleased with her life. But today her self-confidence was shaken. Her mouth was set in a thin expressionless line, and her eyes, which seemed darker than before, avoided contact with his. She had changed, and he had, too. This last month had been hell for them both. "Sarah," he said gently, "I was talking about Sue."

"Yes, Hank. Sue. Where in God's creation? And where's the sugar?" She stood up. "Nothing seems to be where it should be." She groped among the canisters and jars of preserves on the counter.

"It seems you spend your whole life straightening and cleaning," he said. "The house is getting too big to handle."

She turned and looked him straight in the eye. "How does a house grow, Hank?"

"If houses really grew, I'd be out of business."

"In John 14 it says, 'In my father's house there are many mansions.'"

"I thought the word was 'rooms.'"

"'Rooms' in the Standard Revised. 'Mansions' in the King James. I always wondered how a house could have mansions, instead of rooms. But that's how this place feels to me now — the rooms seem huge."

"If a customer told me that, I'd take it as a compliment, but from you..."

"I love this house. You know that. There's nothing like it in the world. I could sit for days curled with a book on that bench in the alcove by the fireplace."

Hank slowly stroked his mustache. "Maybe it's time to think of building another smaller place that would be easier to care for," he suggested. "After all, Russ will be leaving for college next month, and then Fred. Then there will be just the two of us in this big old place. It's time to move on."

"Don't talk of moving," she said quietly, but firmly.

They heard footsteps on the walkway, and both grew tense with expectation. At this time of the morning, it could be either Rem Jones the mailman or the Reverend Schumacher. If it was Rem, there could be another letter from their sons.

Their ten-year-old daughter, Sue, had died suddenly of pneumonia while her two teenage brothers were away camping on their Uncle Harry's ranch in Wyoming. The boys wrote home often, with messages intended for Sue.

There was no telephone at Uncle Harry's ranch, so Hank and Sarah couldn't call and tell them that Sue had died. And Sarah had insisted that a telegram would be too cold and cruel. She had written them a letter, but couldn't bring herself to mail it, though she let Hank believe she had sent one letter after another. Instead, she added to the first, unsent letter each day, and her guilt at not sending it grew as Hank became more and more impatient with the boys for not coming home.

Two days ago, Hank, who was normally cool-headed and practical, threw a screaming fit when another letter from the boys arrived. The unintended irony of their references to Sue pained him, and he lashed out at them.

Sarah found some consolation in that same letter. As long as the boys didn't know, to them Sue was still alive.

The footsteps on the walkway had the light, quick pace of the young Reverend Schumacher.

Hank took a deep breath and sipped his bitter coffee. "Why did I ever let them take the car?" he asked rhetorically.

"It's the only way to get there. You said so yourself. The train would leave them a hundred miles from the ranch, and besides, we simply couldn't afford it."

"Then they simply shouldn't have gone."

"It was time they grew up and learned to go off on their own and rough it. That's what you said."

"And what's the point of their seeing Harry? I know he's your last living uncle, and we can't expect him to live forever. But he'll just fill their heads with war stories — as if they don't get enough of that from the books he sends them every Christmas and birthday, and now the newspapers are full of that new war in Europe. To hear Harry talk, you'd think that war was the greatest thing that ever happened to a man — a chance to see the world and be a man among men. The less we hear from him the better."

At the outbreak of World War I, Harry, at the age of 39, had left behind his wife and children and volunteered to join the American Expeditionary Force under General Pershing. He had received a field commission and, by the end of the war, rose to the rank of captain. After the war, he traveled for two years in Russia, the Middle East and North Africa, purportedly on military-diplomatic missions. He loved to talk about those times and exotic places and to show off the coins, postcards, photos, and artifacts he had collected. But to any question about what he did there, he replied with a wink, "I'm not at liberty to divulge that."

Now, at age 62, Harry lived with his second wife, Martha, age 33, and their three-year-old daughter Matilda, on a large ranch in Wyoming. He named the ranch "Cairo," and in addition to cattle, he raised camels, which he sometimes sold to circuses and zoos, but mostly kept for his own amusement – holding endurance races across the barren plains.

"Harry's harmless," said Sarah.

"Harmless? The man's a dream-maker, and there's nothing in this world more dangerous than that. If it hadn't been for my grandfather and his sand castles, I'd have never ended up a builder."

"And do you regret it?"

"No, but that's not my point."

The Reverend Schumacher, a Lutheran minister, was 25 and unmarried. At first, Sarah had found it difficult to turn for solace to a minister half her age, who had hardly known Sue. But he was so sincere and ardent, she couldn't turn him away. Since the funeral, the Reverend came by nearly every morning to sit with her in Sue's old room, often in silence, but sometimes reading passages from the Bible and then talking about them.

Sarah admired his erudition, his familiarity with foreign languages, and his faith that the words of the Bible are the words of God Himself. It was refreshing to see a young man who felt he had an important mission in life. She hoped he would be able to keep that faith for many years.

Russ was planning to go into the ministry. He'd be starting at Gettysburg College next month, in pre-seminary. Sarah wondered if Russ would ever be this ardent and well-informed. How could her little ragamuffin ever become a "man of God"? To her, regardless of his height (and now he towered over her), he was still a little boy – wrestling with his brother in the backyard and teasing his sister.

The morning sunshine streamed through the window in Sue's room, surrounding the Reverend Schumacher's light brown hair with a halo-like glow. Sarah sat and stared at the miniature horses Sue had arranged on the windowsill, while the Reverend Schumacher considered all the possible meanings of the original Greek New Testament.

Sue had loved horses. She had nearly a hundred miniatures, and on her walls were dozens of pictures of horses, clipped from magazines. One picture, drawn by Uncle Harry, was a pen-and-ink sketch with a horse's skull large in the foreground, lying on a desert plain, and the Rocky Mountains and a herd of cattle in the distance. Sue had had it framed just before the boys went on their trip. Sue had been angry that she, who loved horses, wasn't being allowed to go on this amazing trip to Harry's wild west.

Today, Sarah surprised the Reverend — it was she who had a passage she wanted to understand. "What does the word 'mansions' mean in the King James version of John 14:2, 'There are many mansions in my Father's house'? How can there be mansions in a house? A house is small. A mansion is big. It makes no sense. Why would one translator say 'rooms' and another 'mansions'? What did Christ really say?"

The Reverend Schumacher was delighted that Sarah had asked him. "Christ is speaking to his disciples at the Last Supper. He is telling them about life after death. He is reassuring them that there will be room enough for them in heaven, his Father's house. Perhaps it's meant as an echo of the Christmas story — in heaven there will be room in the inn. But it suggests more than just space in which to live.

"The King James translation just anglicized the Latin, even though 'mansion' has a different meaning in English. The Latin is 'mansio, mansionis,' which means a stay or a sojourn, and, by extension, a halting place, a stage of a journey. Perhaps the passage means that life after death is a stage of a journey; that there are many such stages; that the journey through the house of God is a long one, requiring many rest stops. Perhaps our life here on Earth is just one such stage."

"And what are the words in the original Greek?" she inquired, expecting that the words of Christ would have magical power.

The Reverend quickly consulted the pocket-sized Greek New Testament he always carried with him. "En te oixia tou patros mou monai pollai eisin."

"And what part of that means many rooms or mansions?"

"Monai pollai."

"You mean like 'monopoly'?" she asked.

"That word has different roots, but the Lord works in mysterious ways. Far be it from me to discount the suggestiveness of our living language."

"And the key word is 'monai'?"

"Yes, in the singular, 'mone.' The letters are 'mu omicron nu eta.' It's pronounced like the impressionist painter 'Monet,' or like the French word for loose change – 'monnaie.' It's an unusual word. It's meaning is very similar to the Latin 'mansio.' But, to the best of my knowledge, it has no derivatives in English. Money, monopoly, and monastery all come from different roots. You might say it's a word that died without offspring."

"I often think of my father's house," Sarah said as she stared up at Harry's drawing of a horse's skull. "It was one of those wood-frame houses connected to a barn with a passageway, so you wouldn't have to go out in the snow to get to your horse and buggy. It's still standing – painted blue now instead of white, and they've turned part of the barn into a garage. We lived in the few steam-heated rooms in the center of the house. But in the summer, I spent lots of time in the many rooms of the attic, the barn, and the basement and in the 'secret passageway.' That was what we called the crawlspace under the peak of the roof that led from the barn to the house. I hope that God's house has rooms like that — rooms to go off and be alone in, rooms where you can cuddle up with a good book, big empty rooms you can fill with your imagination.

"These last few nights I've dreamt that there's this secret room where I stored my most precious things — things that have been lost for years: a rusty iron ring a boy gave me in grammar school, a notebook of poems I wrote, and photos of Sam my brother who ran away from home. And last night, it wasn't just the photos that were there, but Sam himself, and Sue, too. Sam and Sue had been playing a game of hide and seek. I just had to find the right room."

Russ and Fred drove up Georgia Avenue, down Blair Road, and past all their friends' houses before parking the olive-green 1938 Nash two blocks from home. They were savoring their final hours of freedom and working out the last details of their grand entrance. They were bringing home a horse's skull — the very one Uncle Harry had drawn — as a present for Sue.

"What if she's over at Nancy's?" asked Fred.

"No chance," answered Russ. "Sue and her friends all sleep late on Saturdays."

"I'd better check those trenches she dug in the woods. That's where she goes on hot summer days like this, to curl up with a book."

"Wake up, Fred. How many times do we have to go over this? It's early in the morning. She's in the house. There's nowhere else she could be. Believe me."

"You're sounding like a preacher already."

"Okay, buddy," said Russ, slapping his brother on the back of the head and parrying a counter slap.

"What if Dad sees me first?"

"Dad probably took the truck. He's probably on his way to a building site by now. If not, he's doing paperwork in the study. Mom's the one to watch for. She'll probably be cleaning up in the kitchen, but she could be anywhere in the house. Your job is to find Sue without letting Mom see you."

"Okay. Okay. Enough is enough."

"Well, tell it all back to me so I know that you know it. What are you going to do once you find her?"

"I'll tell her our coming back early is a secret, that we're going to surprise Mom and Dad. I'll bring her out the side door by the driveway. And you'll be hiding in the bushes with the horse's skull."

"Brilliant. Now go to it, buster."

Fred slipped quietly in the back door of the house and crawled under the dining room table. From under the long white tablecloth, he could see and hear without being seen.

He heard his father's footsteps going from the kitchen to the study and then back from the study to the kitchen; pausing, then going back again and again. Fred had never known his father to pace like that. And where was his mother? She was the one he'd expect to be moving about. Normally, she was never still for a moment — always cleaning and straightening, even while reading a book or talking to a friend. Something felt wrong.

Fred took a deep breath, waited until the footsteps returned to the study, then got up and tip-toed to the alcove by the fireplace. He could hear his father's heavy pacing even louder now.

Carefully, he leaned his head out of the alcove and looked around the living room. Something was missing.

The baby grand piano, the sofa bed, the two stuffed armchairs and the rocking chair were all in place, as before. But on the wall above the sofa, where once there had been a dozen small family photos, now there hung one large photo of Sue. He recognized the pose – it was a formal professional shot, taken last Christmas. But this was an extremely large print – nearly three feet by two feet. The matting and the frame were black.

Fred quietly walked over and knelt on the sofa to get a better look. Inside the glass, against the photo itself, were several newspaper clippings. They were death notices.

Fred heard his own scream before he realized that he was the one screaming, and then he couldn't stop screaming, running across the room, through the hall, tripping over his father, and bursting out the side door by the driveway, still screaming.

Sarah was upstairs in Sue's room, with the Reverend Schumacher. She had heard footsteps in the driveway and once again had tensed, expecting Rem Jones, the mailman. Smiling and pretending to pay attention to the Reverend, she counted to herself. If there was another letter from the boys with no sign that they knew about Sue, she could expect her husband would once again roar with anger.

Instead, she heard a shrill unearthly scream, the sound of running and the side door slamming.

She and the Reverend raced down the stairs and bumped into Hank, who was getting back on his feet and moving toward the door.

Just then, they heard a second scream, almost as loud as the first, and a horse's skull loomed in the window, casting a dark shadow into the hall.

Frightened by Fred, Russ had let the skull fall on his own head. It stuck, blocking his vision; and when he tried to pull it off, the bone dug into his temples and ripped at his ears. He staggered around the driveway in pain, while Fred bellowed incoherently.

Meanwhile, Hank, Sarah, the Reverend Schumacher and Rem Jones watched in shock.

Later, Russ kept asking, "What were the odds?" He, who had never shown any particular interest in math, became absorbed in statistics and probability. He found some kind of comfort in calculating the odds of Sue dying, the odds that all twelve letters their mother had written would get lost, and then that he and Fred would decide to come home unexpectedly.

Every time he calculated the likelihood of three such unlikely events happening at the same time (even if his mother misremembered and it was only ten or even five letters she sent), the probability was one in a number so huge it was beyond comprehension — many times greater than the number of atoms in the known universe.

When Russ told him about these calculations, the Reverend Schumacher said, "The ways of God are mysterious." Russ did not find that answer satisfying. His mind needed something to work on. He didn't want a pat conclusion. He wanted a direction to focus his energy on. If he had been told to say "Hail Mary" a million times, he would have done that. But being a Lutheran, he could find penance and hope of salvation only in working with numbers.

As a freshman at college that fall, Russ found it difficult to focus on his course work — even the math course, which was introductory calculus, rather than the statistics he hungered for.

Meanwhile, at home, Fred took advantage of his parents' new attitude to him as the only child left in the house. He repainted the room he and Russ had shared and rearranged his furniture the way he wanted it. He ate what he wanted, stayed up as late as he wanted, and nobody hassled him about chores or homework. But after a few weeks of what felt like total freedom and self-indulgence, Fred felt restless and dissatisfied.

Before, Fred had always wanted to do things differently than his older brother, but had always buckled under to him when pressured. Now, there was no one for him to react to and define himself against.

One sleepless night, he moved to Sue's old bed and slept more soundly than ever before. Then he started visiting the Reverend Schumacher and spent a lot of time alone in the fields, staring at the sky and the horizon.

For years, he had been determined to go to a different college than Russ and pursue a different career. Now, to his surprise, he felt a growing bond of solidarity with his older brother.

The following fall, he joined Russ at Gettysburg, intending, like him, to become a Lutheran minister.

Pearl Harbor and America's precipitous entry into the war came near the end of Fred's first semester – a time when Russ was close to failing several of his courses.

The war news stirred up memories of Uncle Harry's tales of the Great War and the aftermath in Paris and Constantinople and Cairo. Russ tried to join the Army, but couldn't pass the physical because of flat feet. Fred, who was miffed that his brother had taken that step alone, tried too, and was rejected because of a dislocated shoulder – an old basketball injury.

Russ wrote to Uncle Harry about their problem, and Harry let them know that people were getting into the service who were in far worse shape than they were. He gave them advice on how to get around the bureaucracy.

Sarah and Hank had taken comfort in the knowledge that physical imperfection was likely to save their sons from the war. They were outraged at Uncle Harry's intervention.

Around the same time that Russ and Fred left for basic training, Sarah found out that she, at nearly 50, was five months pregnant. She had gone to her doctor several times, and he had insisted that the discomfort and weight gain she was experiencing were due to change of life. Now, having heard the baby's heartbeat, he embarrassedly changed his story.

Hank rejoiced — it was a blessing from heaven. Sarah considered it an unaccountable burden.

During the last months of her pregnancy, she reread the Old Testament, lingering on the story of Sarah and Abraham and on the Book of Job. She also kept a journal, where she obsessively recorded everything she could remember about Sue, as if memory could resurrect her. On the fly-leaf of that diary she wrote: "Sue died while I was watching. All of a sudden, her body was there, but she wasn't. She — whatever 'she' was — left the body, passed from the room that was her body into another.

"I often dream of houses — huge old houses with secret passages leading to hidden rooms.

"I don't believe in reincarnation. But I do believe there is something else, somewhere else, a hereafter.

"I live in my body. My body is a room I inhabit for a while. And then I pass to another room.

"It's as if Sue lived in a vast house, but she spent all her time in one little room, the size of a closet. And the door was shut. She didn't even know there was a door, until it opened, and she passed from one room to another."

When Charlie was born, he looked so much like Sue that it was painful for Sarah to look at him. Even though money was scarce, they hired a neighbor to help watch him for the first few years of his life.

Meanwhile, the private construction market dried up as the war made building materials scarce and drove up prices. Hank reluctantly gave up his independence and took a job as a foreman on a government project. Around that same time, he found out he had diabetes and had to carefully watch his diet, which added to his growing depression.

For two years, the only good news was the bored and boring letters they got from Russ and Fred, who were stuck at Army camps in the swamps of Georgia and Louisiana. Fortunately, they were never shipped overseas. When they came home on leave, they looked at little Charlie as an unwelcome intruder, to be ignored, at best.

Charlie learned to talk late – no one was listening closely enough to his first attempts to recognize and reinforce the sounds that came close to "mama" and "dada."

By the time he was three, Charlie often tagged along with his father to building sites. He was tolerated as long as he didn't touch anything. He stood, patiently, and watched all day as they dug the foundations, poured the concrete and raised the framework.

Hank was both puzzled and pleased by this quiet, intense interest. Neither of his other sons had ever paid attention to his work. "I wonder what he day-dreams about when he's standing there like that," Hank told Sarah. "What kind of a mansion is he building in that mind of his?"

As soon as the war ended and gas rationing stopped, Hank drove Charlie around Washington, for the pleasure of seeing his wide-eyed reactions to all the sights.

Sarah mocked Hank, "You're old enough to be Charlie's grandfather. That's what you're doing, you know. You're not treating him like a son. You're just enjoying him like a grandson. Lord only knows where he's going to learn discipline and values, the way you spoil him."

That rebuke tickled Hank's fancy and encouraged him to take Charlie on more excursions, especially to the beach in the summer.

When Hank was a child, his grandfather had taken him to the beach at least once each summer. They'd go by train, from Lancaster to Philadelphia and Philadelphia to Ocean City, New Jersey.

Old Grandfather Arnold couldn't swim. The beach, for him, was a place for castles and dreams, and his were not ordinary sand castles. He was a craftsman, a cabinetmaker. He could make wooden pull-toys — crocodiles and bears and elephants that opened their mouths and wiggled their ears and tails when you pulled them. And he made elaborate wood and sand castles on the beach.

All winter long, Grandfather made drawings based on pictures in books of castles in Ireland, Wales and Germany, where his ancestors had lived. He carved and warped pieces of wood until they were just the right size and shape, and prepared all the materials he would need to create those castles in exquisite detail, on the beach.

He didn't want to attract crowds. He'd look for a stretch of beach where there was no one around.

He didn't build them high on the beach, sheltered from the tide. He built them down close to the water, at low tide, and watched with glee when the sea came in and battered those magnificent towers and leveled them just as it did the crude little structures that three-year-olds made.

But that was the point of building on the beach — to watch the waves come, to watch it all get swallowed up, time and time again. Grandfather and Hank would retrieve the wood when the waves started washing it away; and once again, they'd build — the same castle or a new one — at least one for each tide, for as long as they were at the beach.

As long as they had their dreams and their drawings, they could build a new one, as good as or better than all the ones that had gone before. And the sea was doing them a service by erasing them all. In washing the old ones away, the sea was preparing the surface for more castles, and more again.

Now Hank took Charlie to the beach and built sand castles for him near the family cottage on the Potomac. Hank had tried doing that just once before, for Russ when he was three; but Russ was so anxious about the outcome and so respectful of what his father had built that he took the fun out of it. Hank, like his grandfather before him, had built that first castle close enough to the water so nothing could save it. But Russ tried desperately to protect it from the tide. And when the waves won the battle, he sat and cried; and he never wanted to do it again.

Now, on the beach, Hank worked for hours, using all the bits of wood and cardboard he had carefully precut and shaped. Meanwhile, Charlie filled a bucket with sand and turned it over, and did that over and over again, until he had dozens of little towers all up and down the beach, and then ran and kicked them all down, with glee.

When Hank finally finished a huge castle with turrets, parapets, courtyards, and moats with drawbridges, he stood back, proudly, to show it to his son. At that moment, Charlie shouted, "Geronimo!" and belly-flopped right on top of his father's fortress, knocking it flat before the tide had a chance to get to it.

There Hank was – a grown man building a sand castle, and little Charlie by knocking it down showed him in one stroke that he was really doing all this work because that's what he wanted to do – not just to amuse his son. Hank got very mad at Charlie for that, but he loved him for it, too. Charlie got under his skin in a way the other boys never had. They made many such castles together.

CHAPTER THREE
AUNT RACHEL AND THE WIZARD OF OZ

In July of 1946, Russ, recently discharged from the Army in Georgia, arrived home with his new bride, 17-year-old Rachel. He had the cab stop at the corner, and left the luggage there under bush.

Russ paused to admire Rachel. When she was disoriented, as she was now, she looked very young, naive and vulnerable. But alone with him, she had the capacity to turn bold and provocative. He enjoyed comforting her, then shocking her, to watch her switch from one extreme to the other. He was fascinated by this fluctuating, lustful innocence of hers.

He took hold of Rachel's hand and pulled her along, as he slid quickly and quietly toward the house. They stayed behind hedges, ducked behind an oak tree, then dashed to the front door.

"Remember," he told her, "they don't even know you exist. Stay right here. I'll go around the side. It should take five to ten minutes for me to set them up. Then I'll get Mom to open the front door, and you'll say ..."

"Hello, Mom, I'm your new daughter."

"Right. You've got it. The scene will be unforgettable. Just stay put and wait for your cue."

Russ crept back the way he had come, and picked up the suitcases at the corner. Then he strolled casually up the driveway to the side door. He tried to maintain a poker face, but, inside, he was shaking with laughter at this surprise he had prepared for his parents.

He knew they would love Rachel. They would be as delighted as he was that he had been so lucky to meet her and win her. It was as if he had won a million dollars and wanted to spring the news on them with dramatic flare.

And he had another surprise in store for Rachel. He had never told her he had a baby brother. The way she loved kids, she would go wild over little Charlie.

"Mom! Dad! I'm home!" he hollered as he opened the door.

No answer.

"Mom! Dad!" He put the suitcases down and ran to the living room. It was empty.

He hollered even louder, "Mom! Dad!" and rushed into the hall and up the stairs. Still no answer.

He ran back down again, and, winded and disappointed, opened the front door for Rachel.

"Hello, Mom... " she blurted out, then broke into laughter.

"Hush," Russ put a hand over her mouth. "They aren't here. They must be visiting a neighbor. We'll surprise them yet. Come on in. I'll show you around. Then I'll go hunt them down and set them up. Believe me, this is going to work out great. I can't wait to see the look on their faces."

"God!" she exclaimed as she walked in the door.

"Watch your language. How many times do I have to tell you — my parents are touchy about things like that. Never, and I mean never, use the name of God in vain in this house."

"All right, already. But this place is wild. It's just the way you described it." She went straight to the fireplace and curled up on the bench. "Come on over here," she hiked up her skirt above her garter belt and started unbuttoning her blouse. "You know how I've been looking forward to this."

"Not now. They could walk in the door at any moment."

"But we're married," she coaxed. "Remember, anything goes when you're married."

"But not in my parents' house. Besides, there will be time enough for that later."

"Russ, you are simply unbelievable. But I love you anyway." She rushed to him and nuzzled her head into his shoulder. When she stood straight, her forehead was even with his chin.

He slowly ran his hand through her long, straight black hair, and caressed her ears with the large gold-plate loop earrings he had given her. He held her close. "Okay, you little Delilah. We both know you can get your way with me whenever you want. But please don't tempt me now. Come on, I want to show you the house."

He led her upstairs, then had her wait in the hall while he scampered up a pull-down staircase to the attic, and came back with the horse's skull.

"You mean that really happened?" Rachel asked. "That whole wild episode?"

"Of course. And come in here. This was Sue's room. There's the drawing Uncle Harry did of the skull. See, it's a good likeness." He put the skull on the floor in front of the picture. "And over there," he pointed to the other wall, "is that blow-up photo of Sue that spooked Fred when he saw it in the living room."

"God," she started to say, then stopped herself. "Gosh, this room looks like a young girl still lives in it."

"Mom's left everything the same, like she expects Sue to come back some day. From what Dad says in his letters, Mom's gotten superstitious. Every year, on Sue's birthday, she bakes a cake, and sets it up with the right number of candles, as if Sue were still alive and getting a year older each year. According to Dad, Mom claims she has seen the shadow of a young girl a couple times, in this very room, by that very window."

"Oh, I'm so scared of ghosts," Rachel murmured, nuzzling up to him again. "I need a big strong man to protect me." She turned her head to the side so their lips could touch.

He laughed and pushed her back, "Not now."

"But we've never kissed in a haunted house before."

"And you know I couldn't stop with just kissing you. Wait here. I'll go find my parents and bring them back. Then I'll come up and tell you my new plan."

"Why not just tell me now."

"Believe me, if I knew it, I'd tell you. I'll have to figure it out as I go along."

He threw her a kiss from the door.

When Russ first came barging into the house, little Charlie, age four, was playing with tin soldiers in his parents' room. Frightened by the shouting and the loud steps, he crawled under the bed and hid. Then he heard soft voices coming from Sue's room. Then loud footsteps rushed downstairs again.

Slowly, cautiously, Charlie crept out and inched his way toward Sue's room.

Now, standing in the doorway, he saw Sue herself, sitting in her old room, with light streaming through the window behind her.

Her face was in shadow, but even from the doorway he could feel the warmth of her love, a warmth he had never felt before.

She was playing with her miniature horses on the windowsill. He'd never seen a grownup play make-believe before. Her hands slid from one figure to the other as her attention moved. Then she tossed her head back and shook her hair as if she, too, were a horse.

He walked up to her, slowly, without saying a word. He knew without a doubt who she was and presumed that she knew him — after all, he was her brother. Even a ghost would have to know that much.

He was not so much surprised to see her as surprised that it had taken her so long to appear to him.

Charlie tripped over the horse's skull on the floor. The girl turned toward Charlie. Sue had disappeared, and in her place stood another girl, about the same age — a pretty girl, with long black hair. Charlie screamed an unworldly scream, and the girl ran up to him, picked him up and hugged him tight to comfort him.

"Where did she go?" asked Charlie in confusion. "What did you do with her? Where did you hide her?"

"Who?" asked Rachel.

"Sue. My sister. She was just here. You made her go away. Tell her you won't hurt her. Please call her back."

———

Meanwhile, Sarah, walking back to the house from the end of the driveway, saw the shadow of a young girl at Sue's window. She stopped, shut her eyes, turned away, then looked again, and the shadow was still there. She took her glasses out of her pocketbook, wiped them clean on her blouse, and looked again. The shadow was still there.

With trembling voice, she began to repeat the Lord's Prayer, "Our Father..."

Then the shadow moved and an unworldly scream broke loose – Charlie's scream.

Sarah ran up the driveway, stubbed her toe on the doorstep, banged her knee on the screen door, tripped up the stairs and found this strange girl with a wild frightened look in her eyes, holding little Charlie.

The girl hesitated in confusion, then blurted out, "Hello, Mom, I'm your new daughter."

Sarah grabbed a broom from the corner and waved it at her, shouting wildly, "Out, you madwoman, you imposter, you demon."

Rachel instinctively clutched Charlie and ran through the upstairs hall, down the stairs, and out the side door to the driveway.

Sarah came racing after her, waving her broom, and shouting, "Un-hand my son, you, you..."

Rachel cowered, helpless, with her back to the wall. "Your son?" she asked. "But your sons are in the Army, or were in the Army. You're ..."

"Old enough to be his grandmother? Yes, indeed, but he's mine." She reached out her arms to him. He hesitated a moment, then pulled away from Rachel and ran to his mother. She picked him up and hugged him more warmly than ever before. Then she shifted her attention back to the intruder. "And who are you to be playing Goldilocks, wandering into other people's homes?"

"As I tried to explain ..."

"Don't explain anything. Just tell me who you are!"

Rachel hesitated, then answered, "My name is Mrs. Arnold."

"What?"

"Mrs. Rachel Arnold. Mrs. Russell P. Arnold. Your son's new wife."

"Impossible. You're just a girl, no older than..."

32

"Than your daughter Sue would have been? Russ told me about her many times."

Stunned, Sarah simply stared and held Charlie even tighter.

"Russ wanted to surprise you. I thought we should invite the whole family to the wedding, or wait and have the wedding here, or at least tell you what we were doing. But Russ insisted. He's a big kid the way he loves surprises, and I love him for it. He had this whole script he had worked up – what he was going to say to you and Mr. Arnold, and how he'd get you to open the front door and there I'd be standing. But nobody was home when we got here. Nobody except the little one."

"Charlie."

"Yes, Charlie. That must have been another of Russ's surprises – not telling me he had a little brother. That rascal. If I didn't love him so much, I'd hate him," Rachel laughed.

Sarah stepped forward to take a closer look at this girl. Confused and innocent, wearing a plaid skirt and white blouse with saddle shoes and green socks, Rachel looked like a ninth grader just home from school.

Russ emerged from the backyard, walking with his father. "Oh," he stopped short. "I guess you've met already."

"This little girl says she's your wife."

"She most certainly is." He ran up and lifted Rachel, with an arm under her knees and another under her back.

"Is this some sort of joke?" asked Sarah. "She's not old enough to be married."

"She's 17, Mom. In Georgia, that's nearly an old maid. Besides, you were just 16 yourself when you married Dad."

Rachel craned her neck upwards toward Russ, perhaps to kiss him or perhaps to bite him, in anger at the humiliation he was making her go through.

"Seventeen?" repeated Sarah. "Why, Judy Garland..."

"What, Mom?" asked Russ.

"Judy Garland was seventeen when she played Dorothy in the Wizard of Oz. Who could ever imagine Dorothy as a married woman?"

"Oh, that's a wonderful movie!" Rachel nuzzled her head at Russ's neck, all sweetness now. She kissed him behind the ear. "I saw in the paper that it's playing again. When it first came out, I saw it three times and loved it more each time I saw it."

Sarah stared at her, unaccustomed to seeing such open signs of affection. She held Charlie tighter. She was still trying to absorb the shock that Russ was married. "Sue was ten when I took her to it. I haven't been to another movie since. Come to think of it," she added distractedly, "Charlie has never been to a movie at all."

"Oh, but he must go. He simply must," insisted Rachel. "Why that's the most magical movie of all, and movies are the most magical experience on earth. Please let me take him, Mrs. Arnold, please."

Sarah turned now to Russ, now to Hank. She had no idea what to do or say, and she could tell that Russ and Hank were equally confused. Her son had married a puzzling and perhaps wicked little girl. That was an incredible mistake that could throw all of their lives in disorder. But the question at hand was whether to take Charlie to the movies. Sarah felt dizzy. On impulse, she responded, "We'll both take him."

"Great idea," Russ confirmed, with a sigh of relief. "I'll check the times in the paper. That'll give you two a chance to get acquainted while Dad and I catch up and take care of the yard."

"The lawn could certainly use a mowing," added Hank, with a smile.

Sarah smiled too, put Charlie down, and gave him a pat on the behind. "Run on upstairs now, wash up, and put on your best

Sunday clothes. And don't forget to wash behind your ears and under your nails. Let's make an occasion of this — it's not every day you see your very first movie."

Charlie was confused, but he did what he was told. It was bad enough having to get dressed up to go to "God's house" every Sunday. Now he had to get dressed up on Saturday too, to go to some new kind of place. Rachel said that there would be lots of people. And Mom said he'd have to behave and stay still and keep quiet. He hoped this wasn't something he'd have to do again and again, like going to church. He'd rather stay home with Dad and Russ and play and work in the yard. But he knew there was no arguing with Mom.

The building was as big as a church, but instead of wooden benches, there were grownup seats with arm rests. Mom wanted to sit in the back and Rachel up front; so they sat in the back. Then Charlie stood on his seat to see over people, and Mom picked him up, and they all went to the front row.

He was just getting comfortable in his big soft seat when the lights went out. It was darker than nighttime. No light at all. With one hand he grabbed his mother's arm, and with the other he found Rachel's hand. He held his breath and squeezed tight.

Then the curtain opened, and he was almost knocked over with the light and the music. Creatures appeared that were many times bigger than anything he had ever seen before. He wanted to ask, "Which one is God?" But he figured he was supposed to know without asking, and Mom might get upset that he hadn't paid attention in Sunday School.

Rachel gave him a hug, and whispered to him, "They look alive, but it's just a trick. Look up. See that beam of light. That's where they come from. They're just light on a screen. It's nothing to be afraid of."

"Oh, I'm not afraid," he answered, then quickly looked over at Mom to see if she was mad at him and Rachel for talking. But she was just staring at the screen and smiling.

Cartoons switched to news reels, to previews, to a Tarzan serial, to the feature. But to Charlie, it was all one long sequence of pictures — one surprise after another — everyday-looking people and things mixed together with storybook things, like in a dream.

Rachel leaned over and whispered. "I used to live in Kansas. But I never saw a tornado," she added.

"What's a tornado?"

"That is," she said, pointing to the screen, where wind was blowing things every which way.

When the picture switched from black and white to full color, Charlie jumped like he had when light first hit the screen.

Afterwards he remembered Rachel's words more clearly than the words of the movie. And the pictures he remembered best were the ones he saw when she spoke. Years later, he would say that her voice had controlled a camera shutter in his mind. "Ruby shoes ... Munchkins... Scarecrow... Tin Woodman... Lion..." — one snapshot after the other, held forever in memory.

When the Great Oz first spoke, Charlie leaned over close to Rachel and whispered, "Is he God?" But she didn't answer.

The cackling laugh of the Wicked Witch of the West cut right into him. She scared him so hard it hurt. He shut his eyes and tried to think of other things.

He slept through the rest, his scary dreams mixing with sounds and pictures from the movie.

He was glad when it was over and they were safely out on the sidewalk again.

Then Rachel started singing the song about rainbows and Mom joined in. And Rachel took his one hand and Mom the other, and they started dancing and skipping up the street, chanting, "Lions, and tigers, and bears! Oh, my!" It was like they were kids with him or he was a grownup with them. He laughed like he'd never laughed before, and hugged them both with abandon. And they hugged back like he were the most important person in the world and they both wanted him all to themselves.

That day, and every day for a week, Charlie kept talking about the movie and asking questions. Rachel read him the book. Then they went to see it again the next Saturday, and the Saturday after. Gradually, he began to see the story, instead of just pieces. He was fascinated with it, and he loved the grownup attention he got when he talked about it.

"Is our house like that, Mom?" Charlie asked at bedtime. "Can it take us to some other world?"

"Charlie, don't be silly. You know that's just a story, like a dream."

"You mean dreams aren't real?"

"I suppose they're real in their own way. But things aren't just what they seem in dreams. One thing stands for another."

He didn't know what that meant. But he kept asking, "Do you dream, Mom?"

"Of course," she answered. "We all do. That's part of being human — like remembering and building things and talking and reading."

"What do you dream, Mom?"

"Lots of times I dream of houses," she admitted.

"Ones that fly and fall on wicked witches?" he asked.

"No, I dream of this house and the house I grew up in. Sometimes the house has extra rooms — attics on top of attics, and passageways leading to new passageways. Some are empty, and some

37

are storage areas, like at our summer house, with trunks and boxes stacked high. I go wandering through those rooms, from one to another, opening boxes looking for a lost recipe as if the world depended on my finding it. Or I walk into a room that's furnished like a living room, well kept and dusted, with a warm cup of tea sitting on the table, waiting for the owner, whoever she may be, to come back. Or I wake up in a strange bed in one of those rooms, and can't find the passage that will get me out again. Sometimes I think I catch a glimpse of your sister Sue, playing hide-and-seek in those rooms."

"Have you ever seen me there?" he asked.

"No, I haven't seen you in my dreams, and not Rachel — not yet. But I will some day. I'm sure of it. That's the way dreams are."

After that, Charlie made a habit of asking his mother about her dreams when he went to bed at night. Even when she was busy and in a hurry, she would linger a few minutes to talk of that. And his own dreams, instead of jumping from here to there to everywhere, like they had before, began taking shape from pieces she told him — often taking place in huge old houses with unexplored rooms. He was no longer afraid of falling asleep.

CHAPTER FOUR
CHARLIE'S COMING OF AGE

Sarah Brehm was born in 1892 in Plymouth, New Hampshire, a small town where Daniel Webster had lost his first court case, in a one-room schoolhouse that was now the town library. Nathaniel Hawthorne had died there, too, at the Pemigiwasett House — a large white frame hotel, just a block from the Brehm house.

The Brehms had a typical Victorian family — many children and few survivors. Sarah was the youngest. Sam, the sibling closest to her in age, ran away at 12. They heard he got to Boston and took ship, but no one had seen him since. Her sister Margaret became hysterical in her late teens and was put away in an insane asylum, where she died 10 years later. Another brother died of pneumonia. Two others died as infants. Sarah's one remaining sibling — George — volunteered for World War I, and, after the war, settled in New York City, from which he occasionally and unpredictably appeared, bearing gifts.

When Sarah was six, her father and his brother-in-law Harry headed west to see if the prospects there were as good as newspapers and magazines claimed. They spent a year wandering and doing odd jobs on farms in Kansas and Oklahoma.

Harry stayed and had his wife come West to him. But Sarah's father gave up and returned East to his family, to spend the rest of his days working in a shoe factory in Plymouth.

Sarah had met Hank Arnold, her husband-to-be, at the Pemigiwasset House. She was doing maid's work there during summer vacation from high school, and he had come north for the mountain air, on his doctor's recommendation. In late August and September, he suffered badly from hay fever, everywhere but in the mountains.

Aside from his allergies, Hank was muscular and tough – a successful builder who had begun as a construction hand. He was the only son of a Pennsylvania farmer and grandson of a cabinetmaker. Hank wasn't interested in farming. From the day when his grandfather first showed him how to make sand castles using boards for support, Hank had dreamt of building houses – one after the other – whole neighborhoods of houses, teeming with children. After finishing high school, he hiked to Washington, where he found work in the flourishing building trade.

When Hank and Sarah married, he was 21 and she 16. He built a house for them in Silver Spring, Maryland, near Washington, D.C. He also built a summer cottage at Colonial Beach on the Potomac in Virginia.

The cottage was near a lighthouse, across the street from a grove, just above the river bank. The ground sloped upward. In the front, the main part of the building (six bedrooms and the front porch) was on stilts, so it would be protected from high water in case of hurricane. In the back, the dining room and kitchen were at ground level. Under the bedrooms was a storage area, with lattice sides and a dirt floor. Above the bedrooms, accessible with a pull-down ladder, was an attic which could sleep four people in beds and up to a dozen on the floor. In the back, there was a grape arbor, a garage and an outhouse. To the side were a stone-and-masonry goldfish pond and a yard large enough for volley ball, badmitton, and croquet.

When Sarah's Uncle Harry returned from World War I, he stayed at the cottage for an entire summer before heading west. He had volunteered to stay overseas two years after the end of the war, and had just heard from his first wife that she was divorcing him. Day after day, he puttered aimlessly along the beach, heaving stones and shells at unseen targets. Then in the fall, he headed West to start a new life. He left behind several trunks full of military paraphenalia and souvenirs from Europe, North Africa and the Middle East. Those trunks gave the summer house an aura of the exotic.

———————

After taking Charlie to The Wizard of Oz for three Saturdays in a row, Rachel wanted to take him to the cottage, which she had heard about from Russ. Sarah insisted on going too; so Hank took them all.

As soon as the car stopped, Charlie ran out with his bucket and started making quick sand castles along the waterline. Hank followed, making more, then Rachel, then Sarah. Then they all cheered as Charlie ran up the line, stamping on each and every one of them.

Russ watched from a distance. To him, Charlie was still a baby. This four-year-old was a total stranger he didn't know how to relate to. And it was hard to believe that was his fifty-year-old mother, up to her ankles in wet sand, splashing like a ten-year-old.

Not to be outdone, Russ scavenged in the storage area for Uncle Harry's World War I army gear. Then he crept across the street, and hid behind tall grass near the main path. There he set his trap.

When Charlie and Rachel came strolling back up the path, Russ pulled a string, which lowered the grass, revealing what looked like a couple of soldiers, dug in, with guns at the ready. Then he set off firecrackers.

Rachel burst out laughing. But Charlie froze in terror, until Sarah picked him up and raced back to the house to calm him.

"How could you?" muttered Hank in disgust.

The next day, Russ sat on the porch and watched in amazement as, once again, his wife and parents played on the beach like kids. He wanted to join in the fun, but didn't know how except with practical jokes. This time he rigged the house with water balloons. Charlie, who was the first one back, was the perfect victim. Running in through the kitchen door, he was hit by the first, then tripped in confusion and triggered a second and a third. Rachel thought it was hilarious, and this time Charlie laughed too.

After that, Charlie wanted Russ to teach him tricks and surprises that he could play — like short-sheeting beds and putting grapes in slippers. And on cloudy, cool days, the two of them would get out the old army gear and dig foxholes on the beach and in the grove, and play war games with the neighbor kids.

Sarah remembered that summer as the time when she learned to enjoy her son Charlie. She was always grateful to Rachel and Russ for that. But at the same time she felt guilty for feeling so happy, and feared she would never be able to establish the same distance and same level of discipline as she had with her other sons. She was afraid of what might become of him with such an unorthodox upbringing, but she couldn't help but roll in the sand and the waves with him, now that Rachel had shown her what fun it could be.

That fall, Fred got out of the Army and returned to Gettysburg College. He became a Lutheran minister and moved to Illinois, where he married Francine and had two sons – Jimmy and Georgie.

Russ finished college at the University of Maryland, became an actuary for an insurance company, and moved to nearby Rockville, Maryland, where he and Rachel had two sons – Frank and Eddie.

The beach house was where the cousins of the new generation met and played with one another and with their Uncle Charlie.

Charlie didn't really belong in the generation of his brothers or the generation of their children. He was 20 years younger than his brother Russ, and eight years older than Frank, to whom he was more like a big brother than an uncle.

This is where the extended family would gather — some of them for the whole summer, some for weekends, and some just for the Fourth of July. There were plenty of rooms. And when friends and more distant relatives showed up, as they often did, there was always room to spread out more sleeping bags.

This was where Hank got used to being called "Grandpa" and Sarah "Grandma," even by their own sons and daughters-in-law – even by Charlie. It was also where they could still sometimes act like kids themselves, joining Charlie and their grandchildren and their daughter-in-law Rachel to build and break sand castles.

And this was where Charlie could get away with every devilishness he could think up. He was now the practical joker, terrorizing and delighting the young kids. Russ, who no longer indulged in such childishness himself, laughed at and encouraged Charlie's booby-traps and pranks, and prodded his own son Frank to join in.

Charlie also developed an endearing manner with the older generation. When he went too far in his horseplay and was at risk for serious punishment, he could put on a sincere apologetic manner and admit his fault — "everybody makes mistakes" — and nothing came of it.

Once, when Frank was seven and Eddie two, Rachel asked Charlie to babysit.

Russ objected "Charlie at the beach is one thing. But in this house with these kids — that's something else. No way. Absolutely no way."

But the regular babysitter had taken sick, and Rachel was determined to go to this party. There was no choice but Charlie.

"Now look, kid," Russ told him. "To be on the level with you, I think you're too immature for this. Yes, you're 13 years old. Yes, you're tall for your age; but from what I've seen of you over the summer, you're more of a kid than Frankie is. Today I want you to act older than your years, not younger. Surprise me. Show me you can act like an adult."

Charlie smiled broadly — too broadly, Russ would recall — and assured him. "I can act like an adult. Just trust me."

From what Russ and Rachel could determine afterwards, Charlie did indeed fulfill his promise, after a fashion. When they got home, their neighbor Mr. Callahan was waiting on their doorstep; and the house was filled with cigarette butts and empty beer cans.

Apparently, Frankie had woken up, heard laughter and talking in the living room, and peaked around the corner. He saw Charlie with a bunch of older boys — "grown men," he insisted, but they were probably about 18. They were drinking beer and swapping jokes. Frankie didn't understand what they were saying and fell asleep in the hall. When he woke up, the house was dark and quiet.

"Charlie!" he called.

No answer.

"Mommy! Daddy!"

No answer.

Eddie woke up screaming. Frankie panicked and screamed too. Mr. Callahan found Frankie on the sidewalk bawling, "Mommy! Daddy! Where are you?" Mr. Callahan fetched Eddie, too, and brought them both to his house, and left a note on the door.

Charlie came over when he got back. "I thought Frank was asleep," he explained. "I just went out with my friends to get more beer." That explanation from a thirteen-year-old did not go over well with the neighbors.

Russ was furious at the time. But after a few years and many retellings of the tale, even Russ couldn't help but laugh at how Charlie did indeed "act like an adult."

Rachel maintained a special friendship with Charlie. When the family got together, she'd bring him presents, and always had something she wanted to talk to him about — a new movie or book. And Charlie would ask her about her dreams, and record them in a notebook.

Thanks in part to this practice with Rachel, Charlie developed a remarkable ability for getting along with adults. At fifteen, when he was taller than his father, and even a little taller than his brother Russ, Charlie played master of ceremonies at family gatherings — first as a joke, and then as his expected and natural role.

He enjoyed being the center of attention and being in control.

At parties he found just the right words to help strangers mix. At school dances, he made a habit of dancing with all the wallflowers. He was at ease with all girls — bright and dull, beautiful and homely.

By the time he was 18, Charlie was confident enough to practice his powers of flirtation on any woman, regardless of her age. He would give that woman his full interest and attention, keeping her off-balance and animating her, while keeping a respectful distance. This tension of desire and restraint was exciting and liberating – particularly to married women twice his age.

———————

At Colonial Beach, Rachel luxuriated in Charlie's attention. Russ was inclined to get wrapped up in his work and his numbers, and, for weeks at a time, would seem to forget that she was a woman, regardless of her efforts to remind him. At the beach, the attention of this virile and handsome teenage brother-in-law made Rachel feel young again. She wore a revealing two-piece bathing suit that would have scandalized Russ, had he noticed.

She was proud of the figure she had maintained after having two babies. Yes, there were varicose veins on her legs, but a summer tan soon masked those. Strangers found it hard to believe that her oldest son was as old as he was.

On Saturday of Memorial Day weekend in 1960, when Charlie was a high-school senior, Rachel found herself alone with him at the cottage. Everyone else was downtown at a carnival and would be gone for hours.

Rachel could feel the silence in the house as she stood half-naked in her room – the heavy silence, punctuated by footsteps that could only be his, walking toward her door, hesitating, then continuing down the hall, out the door and down the front stairs. She didn't know what she would have said or done if he had knocked or even opened the door.

She felt ashamed of herself for having such thoughts. But yet it gave her pleasure to think that she was that attractive, that he should actually want her physically and have to hold himself back.

She pushed the top and bottom of her bathing suit a bit lower, before she grabbed a towel and ran after him toward the beach.

Charlie was leaning against a pine tree in the middle of the grove. Out of the corner of her eye, she could feel his eyes following her, and she walked with more than her usual sway.

She pretended not to see him and called, "Charlie! Where are you, Charlie? Charlie, did you go off to that carnival and not say a word?"

When he didn't answer, Rachel felt like a mischievous teenage girl. She stretched out her blanket in a sheltered area below the bank, where she couldn't be seen from the road, or from any of the other beaches up and down the river, and just a few feet out of the range of Charlie's view. There she boldly undid the top of her bathing suit and stretched out on her belly to sunbathe.

She heard him take a few steps closer on the bank. She pretended to shut her eyes, but through her eyelashes saw him duck and lie down, hiding behind a bush just ten feet away and gawking at her. She felt deliciously evil. She hadn't felt so desirable and desired since Russ first undressed her fourteen years before.

She sensed he was about to back away, but she wanted this sensuous tension to continue. Smoothly and gracefully, she rolled over, exposing her breasts.

She even dared to look him straight in the eye, very quickly, so he knew she knew, then looked away, not to embarrass him or force him to speak or to leave. She leaned back on her elbows, thrusting her breasts up and forward to grant him a full view.

Rachel and Charlie lay like that, silently for nearly an hour. From time to time, Rachel would change position for comfort, but still give him a picture-postcard view.

Then, still looking away, she stood up, put on the top of the bathing suit and walked back to the cottage as if nothing had happened.

That night, when Russ and Rachel were going to bed, Rachel asked, "What is the probability of a woman becoming pregnant from making love just once without a condom?" As he looked up, she slowly, like a stripper removed her bathing suit, revealing her now suntanned breasts. Her feelings of guilt from her outlandish behavior that morning, added zest to the passion which drew her and Russ together, like a pair of teenagers alone at last after months of groping and lusting. Nine months later, nearly eight years after the birth of Eddie, she gave birth to their third son, Johnny.

That same night, after everyone was in bed, Charlie went out to the beach alone. There, by the light of the full moon, he built a huge and elaborate wood-and-sand castle – using bits of lumber from the storage area under the cottage.

Just after dawn, Hank, on his usual morning walk, found him there. "That's a fine castle, son," he remarked. "I've never seen you do anything like it before. Have you been sneaking down here in the dark to practice?" he chuckled.

"No, this is the first. And it will be the last for a while, too."

"But we have a long summer ahead of us. We could work together on something like that. I'd very much like to, if you'd let me."

"Maybe some other time, some other place," he stared down at his feet. He had come to the beach to be alone with his thoughts. This encounter was unexpected, but Charlie was relieved to have this chance to talk to his father in private. "Dad," he continued.

Hank smiled. "Yes, son."

"I'm joining the Army."

"Well, that's certainly a choice to consider, but I thought you had your heart set on college in the fall," Hank responded in a friendly, but patronizing tone. "Let's talk about the army in a few weeks, after you've graduated from high school. Then we can weigh all the pros and cons together."

"No, Dad. I've made up my mind. I'm not going back to school. I'm not going to take finals. I'm not going to graduate. I'm simply going to join up. Please don't try to talk me out of it," he quickly added. "It was a difficult decision. Please don't make it any more difficult."

"But why are you doing this, Charlie? What's your dream?"

"I've got lots of them, Dad. Maybe that's the trouble – there are so many dreams floating around in my head that I don't know which one is really mine. Maybe I'll become a builder like you, or a soldier like Uncle Harry, or a minister like Fred. Or maybe I'll write books or make movies. I can see myself doing any of those things. But mostly, I see myself with women – almost every woman you can imagine. And that just makes everything confused. I need to get away and sort it out before I make a total mess of things."

"Well, Charlie, I hope you do sort things out. Most folks never do." Hank shut his lips tight. He looked long and hard at the sand castle, then simply sat on it, making himself comfortable, as he knocked over towers and walls. Charlie laughed and sat beside him – it was a very big castle.

"You know, I don't talk much," said Hank. "Your mother's the one for words. But this sand castle of yours has got me to thinking. What I mean to say is – I like to think that what matters is what you do, more than what you say. I like to think that what I do with my hands is what makes me who I am. I like to be in control. But time and again, I see dreams and stories and ideas making more of a difference than just plain facts. I can't make sense of it, but it happens even to me. Why am I a builder?" he asked Charlie.

"I suppose because you wanted to be one."

"Yes. And why did I want to be one? Where did the motivation come from? It was a dream, planted in my mind by my grandfather, the cabinetmaker. And Russ and Fred joined the Army in wartime, when they didn't have to, because of a dream their Uncle Harry had planted in their heads. And there are plenty more dreams floating around in this family, just waiting to be picked up by somebody else and change their life around."

"What do you mean, Dad?"

"I think of your mother and those house dreams she's always telling you about, and all her superstition about death not really being the end of things. I think about Russ and the way he liked to set up surprises — like what matters isn't what you do, but how you let everybody know about it; like it's okay to marry a girl you hardly know, if you can make a good story out of it. That's the kind of thing I'm talking about.

"Dreams like that can have a life of their own. They seem to move from person to person, from generation to generation, living and growing and changing.

"There's something risky and uncontrollable about them. I don't trust the way they can change your motivation and make you go in a direction that nobody would have expected from the plain facts of the matter."

Charlie took a board from the castle and heaved it side-arm so it skipped on the water like a large flat stone, then floated on the waves. They watched it quietly for a few minutes before Charlie answered, "It isn't a dream that's making me do this, Dad. I don't have some ambition to push me in one direction. No, I'm doing this because I don't have a direction and need to find one."

"But you dropping out of high school when you're nearly done, and not going to college — for now at least — that feels so much like me at your age, when I left my father's farm and went to Washington to become a builder. That made no sense to my father, just like this makes no sense to me now.

"Don't get me wrong, son. I know you need a sense of direction. I know you need to figure out who you are and who you want to be, and you need to follow through with what you promise yourself. But I'm scared, son. I'm scared of what dreams can do to a person. Please don't build your life on dreams.

"But how can I tell you straight, when it isn't straight in my own mind," Hank continued. "I loved building sand castles with my grandfather. And I loved showing you how to do it. I'm a dreamer, too. I suppose that's part of being a builder — you don't make houses with just boards and bricks; you need plans, patterns, ideas, dreams to give them a shape so they can fulfill a purpose. But my advice is — stay in control. Keep your sand castles at the beach. That's where they belong. That's the only place where building and breaking bring no harm to anyone."

CHAPTER FIVE
RECRUITED

The recruiter's office was a large closet, with one small table and two chairs. It was a temporary space in the Post Office building, shared with a dozen other organizations. The Army recruiter had it Tuesday and Thursday from 3 to 5 PM.

Charlie stopped in the doorway and looked around. The walls were covered with gray paint, which was peeling in large strips near the one window on the street side. There were no posters. There wasn't even a rack with brochures. The recruiter, in well-pressed dress greens, with highly polished buttons, was hunched over the table, absorbed in a paperback book. His name tag read "Sergeant Camaratta." There were two uneven stacks of books on either side of him. Each book had one or more bookmarks sticking out from the pages.

Charlie had never been to a job interview. For summer jobs, he worked on construction projects for his father or his father's friends.

Standing here, quietly waiting, he was apprehensive, but he was proud of himself, as well. He was taking charge of his life with this bold dramatic gesture.

He expected to have to go through a brief, painful period of transition, like diving into the river on a cold morning. Once he was in, he was sure he would do fine. Millions of others before him had gone through basic training and a three-year hitch in the Army. He was in good physical shape. He would do fine. He just wanted to sign up and get it over with.

Charlie's feet itched. He could smell his own sweat.

The sergeant kept reading with a frown of intense concentration. He was heavy-set, with a square pock-marked face. His hair was cut short and flat like a well-trimmed hedge. Only when he got to the end of the chapter, marked his place with a torn piece of paper and reached for another book from the stack to his right, did he acknowledge that Charlie was standing there.

"Hello, son, what can I do for you?" asked the sergeant.

"I want to sign up."

"Fine. And what do you want to do?"

"Like I said – I want to sign up."

"Yes, son, but are you interested in the Army as a career or are you looking for a chance to learn skills that will help you get a job in civilian life?"

"Mister, to be honest, I don't know what the hell I want to do. That's why I'm here."

"Okay. Let's start with first things first. How old are you?"

"Eighteen."

"Have you graduated from high school?"

"No."

"How far did you get?"

"Mister, you're not making this easy for me. I was supposed to graduate in two weeks, but I just dropped out."

"Kicked out?"

"No, dropped out. My grades were okay. I was planning to go to college. But I just can't keep going like I've been going. I don't like myself any more. I need to get away. I need time to figure out who I ought to be and how to get there."

"Hey, kid, don't we all? But what's the rush? Believe me, you're going to need education to get anywhere. Go ahead, put up with another two weeks of high school. Then put in a few years in the Army, see something of the world, grow up a bit. Then you can come back and really get something out of college."

"Mister, please. I don't give a damn about college. Sign me up and get it over with."

"Just a second, kid. What's your hurry? Do you see a long line of people waiting behind you? Let's do this right. Whatever you do, do it right. Now, what subject turns you on?"

"I was thinking of maybe becoming a builder like my father or a minister like my Uncle Fred."

"Listen to the question kid — at school, what subject really grabs you?"

"I don't know. I might end up writing books or making movies or just stay in the Army. How can I know until I try it?"

"You do have trouble listening, don't you? Well, look, kid, don't you ever want to read Finnegan's Wake or understand quantum physics?"

"What the hell is Finnegan's Wake?"

"I never read it myself, never could finish it, that is. But if you like to read — and the way you keep looking at those books, you probably do — then that's probably the biggest challenge there is. Do you like challenges, kid?"

Charlie stared in disbelief. He had never imagined that something so simple as volunteering for the Army could be this difficult. Instead of being allowed to dive, he was forced to stand on the dock, getting splashed repeatedly, with a chill wind blowing. He felt small, young, and unsure of himself.

He was vulnerable, and the recruiter was taking advantage of him, lording it over him, lecturing at him.

"Who or what are you running away from?" asked the Sergeant. "Did your girlfriend dump you? Did you get some girl pregnant? Are you in trouble with the law? Look kid, this isn't the French Foreign Legion. This is the peacetime Army."

Charlie raised and lowered his hands twice, as if he were trying to talk with them and had forgotten how. Then he grabbed hold of the back of the empty chair and said, "I'm not trying to sign up for the Marines. I just want to join the Army. Will you give me the papers to sign and get it over with?"

"Wake up, you smart ass," answered the recruiter. "Get your shit together."

Charlie let go of the chair and turned around, toward the door. He wasn't used to hearing adults use language like that. Without looking at the Sergeant, he shot back, "I didn't come here to get interrogated – I just want to join the fucking Army." He was trying hard to sound tough, but the word "fucking" came out mumbled.

The Sergeant continued, "Didn't your father sit you down and tell you you're acting like an asshole? Go finish high school. Then come see me."

Charlie turned back, and grabbed the chair again, "I've made my decision."

"But there's more than one decision to make."

"What?"

56

"When you are drafted, you have little or no choice. But when you enlist, you get to choose your MOS, your Military Operational Specialty — provided you can pass whatever test is involved."

"I don't want to choose."

"You have to choose."

"Just pick one for me at random."

"Look kid, this is my job. I take pride in my job, and I do it well, even when idiots like you don't give a damn."

"All right, all right. I'll pick one at random. Then just sign me up and get me out of here."

"It's not that simple, kid. First you take the physical. We could schedule that for tomorrow. Then you pick your MOS. Then we give you tests. Then we schedule your training. The basic training is easy to schedule, but some of the specialty schools have few openings and only start once or twice a year. We'll want to schedule your stint at basic training so that when you get out, you can go straight to AIT, Advanced Individual Training."

"But why?"

"Because I've got a heart and a head, kid. Because that's the way it should be done. Because no one in their right mind wants dead time between training. Believe me. You don't want six months of nothing but polishing your boots and waiting to be put on KP or any other shit duty that happens along."

"But I don't want to sit around waiting for training to be scheduled. What's the point of waiting? I would have graduated in two weeks."

"That's fine. Get on back to school. We'll build that into the schedule. You can sign up now and graduate with your class."

"Don't you understand? I don't want to graduate. I've made a decision and I'm going to stick to it. I've made a decision and I want to get on with it as soon as possible."

"Life just ain't that simple, kid."

It took Charlie a couple hours to walk the ten blocks home.

"I kept supper warm for you," his mother offered hesitantly as Charlie shuffled by.

"Thanks, Mom. But I'm not hungry."

"Did you... Did you actually do it?" she dared to ask.

"Yes and no," he mumbled. "It's complicated. I'll take the physical tomorrow." He dragged his feet as he walked up the stairs.

Sarah and Hank had decided not to challenge him on this. They knew that overt resistance would make him more determined. They hoped that if they didn't make an issue of it, he might come to his senses and return to school in time to graduate.

Charlie shut the door to his room, pulled down the shades, and collapsed on his bed. He felt weak and tired. He just lay there, his eyes shut, trying to fall asleep.

When he opened his eyes again, the room was dark, and he was neither awake nor asleep, but trapped in some restless in-between state.

Moonlight shown through the shades. He could make out the familiar shadowy shapes of his bureau, desk and bookcases. He thought he was awake, but he couldn't move his head or his body, only his eyes. He scanned the room, anxiously, for what might appear. He was an avid recorder of dreams, but this wasn't like any dream he had had before.

On the far wall, between the windows, where no outside light could shine, purplish blue light appeared, as if a movie projector had been turned on, sending a beam of light against the wall as a screen. As he looked more closely, he realized that there was a range of colors, going from light blue at the top and fading into dark purple toward the bottom.

His every muscle was tense. His calves spasmed in cramps, but he couldn't move his legs and couldn't scream.

Against that blue-to-purple background, a picture began to move upward into view, like a scroll unwinding. A white sleeve, as from a toga, appeared. Then came the shoulder, and he knew, while he was watching this vision, that that was the arm and shoulder of Jesus Christ.

He saw himself step forward and kneel, with head bowed low, before Christ. He felt the coolness of Christ's shadow where his bare knees met the gravel of the street.

There were many people around, but he didn't dare raise his head to look. They were speaking a language that he didn't understand, but he knew that he could make three wishes.

He tried to say, "Fame, fortune, and love." But his tongue and lips were numb and unresponsive, like from Novocain at the dentist. The once-in-a-lifetime chance would pass. With heroic effort, he forced out the words as loudly as he could. With horror, he woke to his own voice shouting, "Aunt Rachel!"

The light vanished.

A fly was buzzing, caught between the shade and the windowpane. It was a loud buzzing – loud enough to wake people in the next room or down the hall, and they'd come running, wondering what was going on, why he was shouting his Aunt's name in the middle of the night.

He opened the window and let the fly out.

Then he lay still, trying to conjure once again that image of Christ.

The wall remained dark and blank.

When he got up the next morning, Charlie recorded this vision in his journal of dreams. He didn't tell his mother or anyone else about it. He was convinced that he must start his life anew, and didn't want to give anyone an opportunity to talk him out of it.

He had to let go, to abandon control, to open up and be more aware and considerate of other people. Strangely, joining the Army was the first step in that direction.

As a test of his resolve to become a new person, he would go ahead with his decision. He would quit school, without graduating, and join the Army — even though he realized it was irrational, even foolish.

He would humble himself. This was an act of self-denial, a religious penance that he took on with youthful fervor and pride.

When Charlie entered the recruiter's office for the second time, he noticed not just the books, but also the titles and authors. There were several novels that had come out over the last few years: Dr. Zhivago by Pasternak, Exodus by Uris, On the Beach by Shute. In addition, there were works of Plato and Aristotle, a Bible, the Book of Mormon, a dog-eared copy of Finnegan's Wake, and a German-English dictionary. The book Sergeant Camaratta was reading was in a foreign language.

"Excuse, me, sir," Charlie dared to interrupt. "What's that book?"

"Der Schloss in German," he answered with a smile. "In English it's The Castle, by Kafka."

"How did you learn to read German?"

"I taught myself," he answered proudly, "while I was stationed in Germany."

"And can you actually read this many books in a day?" Charlie asked in a tone of sincere admiration.

"No, not in a day. I read a chapter of this, then a chapter of that. That's my style. Some folks would be bored out of their minds with an assignment like this — recruiter for the peacetime Army. But I love it. It gives me lots of spare time to improve my mind." Seeing the kid was interested, he continued. "I'm not a college type myself. I taught myself everything from science to languages to history to literature.

"There's nothing sacrosanct about going to college," he added. "If you like challenge and drive yourself and work hard, you can learn a hell of a lot on your own. What matters is what you know and what you do with what you know, not how many degrees you have. But from what I've seen, college is good for a lot of guys. It makes learning a lot easier if you can afford to set aside four years to do nothing but study. I never had that luxury myself. I wish I had. Don't pass up your chance, kid."

"I know you're right," admitted Charlie. "But I also know I have to do this."

"Okay, kid. Then let's fill out some forms and take some tests."

———————

Two hours later, as the Post Office was closing, the Sergeant was rechecking the test answers for the third time, scratching his head, and glancing now and then out the window. Finally, he said, "Look, kid, I don't know if anybody's ever told you — but you've got smarts. I've never seen results like you got on those tests. Look, I think I can do something for you. What do you think of languages? Radio? I just saw an opening for a Russian language specialist, 98G."

"But I don't know Russian."

"That's the point — these tests say you have talent for languages, so much talent that the Army will send you to school — to the Defense Language Institute in Monterrey, California, for a full year of training. Then you'll go to Goodfellow Air Force Base in Texas to learn how to listen in on Russian radio transmissions."

"What's the catch?"

"Yes, there is a catch. Together with basic, that's nearly two years of training. If the Army is going to invest that much in you, they want to get payback. So you have to sign on for four years, instead of the usual three."

"And where would I be stationed."

"Any of about a dozen places overseas. Most likely in Germany."

CHAPTER SIX
THE PICTURES FROM CHARLIE'S WEDDING

"Probably got some girl in trouble," Russ concluded when he first heard Charlie had joined the Army without finishing his senior year of high school.

Russ disapproved of almost everything Charlie did. He resented the fact that his parents treated Charlie so differently than they had him and Fred. He believed that Charlie was spoiled and insisted that he wouldn't raise his own son that way, even though Rachel was inclined to. He would rely on old-fashioned discipline, and it was just as well Charlie was gone because he wouldn't want his son Frank to come under his influence.

Frank, who was 12, didn't much care what his uncle did. He was caught up in Little League – he had finally made the "majors." Then, in July, his family moved to Philadelphia. Frank hardly noticed that Charlie was gone.

After basic at Fort Bragg in North Carolina, Charlie came back for a few days at the end of summer. Frank saw him at the beach on Labor Day.

Charlie brought a super-8 movie camera, and all day he shot roll after roll of film of the family and the cottage. Everybody went out of their way to dress up — especially Rachel, who changed three times in one afternoon. Frank had never experienced anything like this before. He showed off and made faces in front of the camera as often as he could, and anxiously waited for nightfall, when Charlie was going to show some movies.

"You won't be in the movies you see tonight," Charlie explained. "I'm not a miracle man. It takes a week to get the film developed."

"But these are real movies, aren't they?" asked Frank.

"Yeah, sure. A real imitation of life."

"I've never seen 'home movies' before — just the junk they have in movie theaters and on TV."

"That's not junk kid. That's the kind of stuff I'd like to be able to make."

"Come on, Charlie. You're the greatest. You always will be," Frank insisted.

But when he saw the movies that night, with the rest of the family, he had his doubts.

Hank hung a sheet from the clothesline out by the goldfish pond. Rachel dressed up like she was going to a Hollywood premiere. And Sarah popped pop corn.

"These are shots from the last few days of basic training," Charlie explained. "I'd just gotten the camera and was experimenting with light."

The movies went on and on. There was no sound — just light flashing and guys in uniforms running around. Frankie fell asleep long before it ended.

Next August, Charlie returned on leave again after nearly a year at the Defense Language Institute in Monterrey, California. Now he always had a book in his hand – either in Russian, which he was studying for the Army, or in German, which he was studying on his own, or about chess, which he had learned from his bunkmate.

Charlie still had his 8 mm camera, but he was much more deliberate in his use of it.

Frank's baby brother Johnny was taking his first steps. Charlie had Rachel pose with Johnny, standing him up, moving away and holding out her arms for him to run to her. Johnny just stood there confused by the camera and all the people, then fell down on his bottom and cried.

Rachel held out her arms, coaxing and encouraging him. But Russ lost patience, swooped down, picked up the crying baby and deposited him in Rachel's lap.

"Terrific!" shouted Charlie. "I couldn't have scripted it better."

Charlie asked Frank to gather all the kids he could find. Then he filmed them as they ran this way and that, following his directions. Frank couldn't see any point or purpose to it.

The Navy was testing new weapons at Dahlgren across the river in Virginia. Charlie was delighted at this opportunity for "realism." He filmed the kids running up the beach, jumping to avoid stepping and slipping on the dead fish that had washed ashore.

Sometimes he let Frank hold the camera and got into the action himself, telling Frank exactly what to shoot and how.

Then he took individual shots of everyone in the family waving their arms in odd ways.

The next day, Charlie drove to the University of Maryland, where a friend let him use the lab to develop the film and edit it.

That night the family gathered once again by the goldfish pond to see this strange new creation.

Before starting the projector, Charlie played a record with loud electric guitars and words that no one could decipher.

Entitled "Arms", this silent movie began with Rachel reaching out her arms to Johnny. Johnny fell down. Rachel reached again and again. Johnny fell again and again, until he screamed and Russ snatched him up.

Then a woman's arm appeared. Naked to the shoulder, it reached out and gestured, "Please come." Then another arm patted a puppy. Another waved good-bye.

Another appeared suddenly, sticking out a thumb to hitchhike, only to be pushed aside by another with an abrupt "stop" gesture.

Then a fist was raised high in protest, and another and another, one of which turned to an obscene gesture, followed immediately by an older woman's hand from the other side of the screen, with a finger waving "naughty, naughty," then "no, no," and finally pointing forcefully in accusation.

Charlie himself appeared in the movie, all alone in a field. He pretended his hand was a pistol and practiced drawing it and firing. He set up a can and stepped back with his hand in holster position. He pretended to draw and fire. Nothing happened to the can.

He drew and fired again. This time the can jumped as if hit with a bullet. The punctured can lay on the ground.

The focus shifted back to his hand as he held it close to his face, staring in surprise. He pointed the finger toward his head, then warily pointed it away.

He set up another can, drew again, and fired again.

Once again the can was hit with a bullet.

Proudly, he blew on his finger as if blowing away smoke, then polished his finger on the sleeve of his shirt.

He swung in a circle, aiming at possible targets. A group of kids, including Frankie, was standing in the far distance, out of focus. Charlie raised his finger-pistol, aimed and pretended to fire at the group – "bang-bang."

Frankie dropped. Charlie grinned proudly.

Some kids in the group gathered around Frankie's body. Others looked around bewildered. One, then two, then three of them started gesturing angrily in the direction of the gunman. Charlie tried to look innocent, put his hands in his pockets, whistled, and turned to walk toward the camera.

He looked back and saw the group was running after him. He started running away from them, toward the camera.

The group was getting closer. They were visible over his shoulder. He pointed his finger back and "shot" while he ran. Several kids fell as if hit by bullets.

They were gaining on him. Charlie stopped and fired several times. Several more of the group fell, but there were even more kids chasing him now.

They all raced up the beach, dodging the dead fish.

They were just about on top of him. He dropped to his knees and covered his eyes with his hands.

A subtitle appeared: "Lord, please let this be a dream."

The kids swarmed over him angrily, blocking him from view.

When the group backed away, Charlie had no arms, just the empty sleeves of his coat.

He squirmed on his back on the ground.

A subtitle appeared: "Disarmament."

Then another subtitle: "Violence is as much a part of us as our arms."

His curled-up body filled the frame.

The kids pointed menacingly at him. They started to close in on him.

His eyes were shut. He was cringing in fear. Then he opened his eyes like he had an idea. He raised his right leg and started to swing it in a circle while lying on his back. He shook his leg as if it were a machine gun firing. Each member of the group fell in a row as if hit with a bullet from the leg.

He laughed hysterically in the middle of a circle of bodies.

Frank applauded wildly and insisted on seeing it three more times. He hadn't the faintest idea what it "meant." But it looked like a "real" movie. And he himself was in it, and he himself had helped to shoot it.

Frank didn't see Charlie during his brief visit home six months later, before leaving for Germany.

By the time Frank saw another Charlie movie, it was the summer of 1963. In the meantime, the Berlin Wall had been built, Yuri Gagarin had orbited the Earth in a satellite, and Kennedy and Khrushchev had brought the world to the brink of nuclear war over Cuban missiles.

This film arrived by mail from Germany with special instructions from Charlie not to look at it until all the family was gathered. Sarah and Hank invited everyone to the beach for a special showing on a sheet by the goldfish pond.

There was an audio tape in the package that had to be played in sync with the film. According to the instructions, everyone was supposed to stay quiet until it was over.

The film opened with shots from home movies of family gatherings that they had seen before. But the audio tape gave them a different dimension, because they were hearing the voices of other people watching these same movies and reacting to them. The voices on the tape were like voices of other people in the same room with the people watching this film now.

The reactions were familiar and natural – how cute the babies were, how much Eddie and Frank and their cousins had grown, how cousin Matilda had put on weight, how young Aunt Martha looked back then. Then there were shots of the whole family at the airport, gathered to see Charlie off, after his last leave, when he went off to Germany.

Charlie never appeared on screen. He was the eye of the camera. People talked to him and waved to him. He just kept shooting.

Now the shorts were of Europe – Munich, Heidelburg, Paris, Geneva. Two of the voices in the background said that they had been to those places before, just like Fred and Francine, who were actually in the room watching it during this first showing. Charlie had not only guessed the kinds of things they would say, but had also mimicked the rhythm of their speech and the tone of their voices.

The character in the film was named "Charlie" – for this was a film with a story, and not just, as we had been led to believe, another showing of home movies. The Charlie in the film had always wanted to be a movie director, but his father had insisted that he become a lawyer. That was a bit of fiction. Hank had never expressed an opinion on what Charlie should become.

The father on the tape, was proud of his son, proud that he had gone to college (which the real Charlie hadn't), proud that he had been through ROTC and gotten a commission, proud that when he got out he would go to law school, following in his father's footsteps.

The Charlie in the movie had a girlfriend, Holly – a doctor's daughter, who lived a few blocks away. She was a charming girl, who always smiled the same sweet smile.

Holly, chaperoned by an aunt, had come to Europe to visit Charlie. They were due to get married back in the States next year. This summer he was using his Army leave to show her around Europe.

Then one of the unseen voices in the movie — a little kid — asked, "Who's that other girl?"

"What?" asked the grownups in the movie.

"The one with the short blond hair. There she is again."

"Yeah," replied the voice of a teenage boy. "She's been in nearly every one of the shots from Europe, standing in the background."

Then she appeared alone on a hillside, tossing her hair in the wind, picking wildflowers and throwing them at the cameraman. After a few seconds, the film cut back to Holly and her aunt at an outdoor restaurant in Paris, then to the stranger on the hillside again.

After that, it was impossible not to notice this stranger, in every scene. More and more frequently, the camera would stray from Holly and linger on the stranger. Sometimes the stranger would pay no attention to the camera. Other times, she would wink slyly.

Then the screen went blank, and the audience heard the voice of Charlie himself for the first time. He said how important his family was to him, how he loved them all, how he had always struggled to live up to their high expectations of him. At first, it was hard to tell if he was talking to his family directly and truthfully or if this was part of the movie.

"I want to apologize," he went on. "You all had such wonderful hopes and plans for Holly and me. I wanted to give you the pleasure of sharing in my happiness. But love doesn't follow timetables. When you've met the woman of your dreams, a year is simply too long to wait."

The film started again. It was a church, crowded with people. The camera — Charlie's eye — was in the front near the altar. He looked around, quickly, nervously — handheld camera effects. Finally, the camera turned and aimed at the bride as she walked up the aisle. She was out of focus, then in focus very briefly, then out of focus again. Then she was next to Charlie in front of the altar; and, in sharp focus, it was clear what everyone had begun to suspect – he was marrying the stranger, the girl with the short blond hair.

The credits came on, superimposed on her playful, smiling face, as they took their vows at the altar.

Produced by Charlie.

Directed by Charlie.

Starring Charlie and Irene Arnold.

Awarded third prize at some film festival in Germany.

That was the first time anyone in the family had heard of Irene.

Eddie and Frank thought that film was a "class act." They wanted to see it over and over again. As they watched it, they paid special attention to this mysterious and lovely older woman. The movie and this new woman raised Charlie even higher in their opinion. They feared him, envied him, and held his every word in special reverence.

CHAPTER SEVEN
IRENE IN MUNICH

On his first weekend pass, Charlie and two Army buddies — Max and Griff — took the train from Augsburg, where they were stationed, to Munich. They checked into the Drei Lowen Hotel near the station. Max and Griff headed straight for the red-light district. But Charlie, map in one hand and small satchel in the other, strolled through the cobblestone streets of the medieval center of the city at Marienplatz toward the district of Schwabing, the English Garden and Schellingstrasse. His goal was the Schelling Salon, a gathering place for chess players.

He paused before opening the door, expecting to find here the "true Germany," not just another Americanized beer-joint full of homesick GIs.

The round tables of the huge room were crowded with young and old adults, mostly men. The lights were dim. Cigarette smoke hung like a thick fog. "Was wollen Sie?" asked a hard-faced waitress in a black skirt with white blouse.

"Essen, bitte," he replied in an unmistakable American accent.

73

She looked not at his face, but at his insignia of rank — a lowly Spec 4 — then reluctantly led him to the one empty table in the center of the room. She didn't seem pleased to have to serve an American GI, much less an enlisted man. She handed him a menu, then disappeared into the smoke and the crowd.

None of the other patrons were eating. Most were drinking beer or coffee and talking loudly. There were a few chess players at tables in the corner, with kibitzers leaning over their shoulders.

He studied the menu and, with the help of a pocket dictionary, decided to order a beef stew dinner. But the waitress was nowhere to be seen.

He felt awkward — the only soldier, the only American, and probably the only person in the place ordering dinner.

He was tempted to go over to the chess players and watch, in hopes of playing in a few games himself. But he didn't want to leave the table for fear of missing the waitress, who sooner or later must remember him and return for his order.

He looked up every word that he didn't know on the menu — dozens of words. And still the waitress didn't appear.

Finally, he opened up his satchel, took out his chess pieces and board and a well-worn copy of My System by Aron Nimzovitch. No sooner had he set up the pieces, than the waitress reappeared.

She reached out her hand and said emphatically, "Funf Marken." Confused, he picked up the menu again and, reluctant to botch the German pronunciation, pointed to the item he wanted.

"Ja, ich verstehe. Aber hier Sie Schach spielen und das funf Marken kostet."

Charlie looked again at the menu. The item he had selected had a price of 20 marks and she was saying something about 5 marks. He was afraid she had misunderstood his order. He pointed again.

Again she said, "Funf Marken fur Schach spielen." Her tone implied he was acting like an idiot.

"Excuse me, but I don't understand. Do you speak English, please?"

She glared at him as if grossly insulted, then knocked over the pieces.

He leaned over and caught the queen before it hit the floor. As he sat up again, a young man in a black jacket and cap at a nearby table handed the waitress some coins, then she walked away.

"Please excuse her," the stranger said. "She speaks not English."

"Thank you. How much do I owe you and what was that all about?"

"Five marks. They cost here five marks chess to play. Rent for the table."

"But I ordered supper," he explained while repaying him. "That costs far more than five marks. And I only set up the pieces for myself, to go over games from a book."

"Yes, and she supper will bring. But chess to play five marks costs. One rule for all... Would you like chess to play?"

"Why, yes," Charlie admitted.

"Sehr gut." The young man took off his jacket, hung it on the back of a chair and sat down. When he took off his cap, long blond hair descended to his shoulders.

At that moment, even with the bad lighting and the smoke, it became clear that the stranger was really a young woman, with deep blue eyes.

"You know how to play?" Charlie asked in surprise.

"A little," she smiled. "Women in America do not chess play?"

"A little. I mean, not very well. I mean, not very many."

"Yes, it is a man's sport," she took the king from his hand and hefted it. "The pieces are so heavy. You from America come. You Bobby Fischer know, yes?"

"Yes, everyone knows ..."

"You play with him often?"

"Never, I mean, yes, of course," he boasted and smiled back.

"Then you must play very well, yes?"

"Well, I have been known to win a few games."

"Sie sind Grossmeister, ja? I can from your eyes see you great depth of mind have. Your eyes, they are dark blue, like mine, yes?"

"Yes," he said automatically. He would probably have said "yes" to anything she asked. He had no control over the situation and didn't like being out of control. But despite himself, he was reveling in the attention of this intriguing young woman.

She set up the pieces and asked "Time? You the time have?"

"Of course," he answered. "Lots of time."

"Die Uhr, die Schach Uhr, bitte? The clock, yes?"

"Yes, of course. It's three o'clock." He showed her his watch.

"One moment, please." She got up and disappeared into the crowd.

He wondered what mistake of language or local courtesy he had made this time.

A few minutes later the blond returned with a clock that had two faces. She set it down beside the board and pushed one of the two buttons on top.

He stared at the clock and at her, wondering what was expected of him.

"The move, it is yours," she said, gesturing toward his pieces.

"Of course." He quickly moved his king pawn forward one square.

She stared at the board, then at the clock, then at him. "The time," she gestured.

"Yes, of course." He hadn't the faintest idea what she was talking about.

"Push the time, the button." She pushed the button on his side of the clock then quickly made her move.

He tried to concentrate on the board. His eyes were watering from the smoke in the air.

"Solch ein grosser Grossmeister. Many times you this book of Nimzovitch read? – a very great book."

"Yes, I mean, not really. I bought it second-hand. I haven't gotten that far. It's quite complicated."

"Ja wohl. Play you for money in America?"

"Yes, of course. Sometimes. It can make the game more interesting."

"Play you now for money?"

"Yes. Why not?"

"Ja. Why not?" She put five marks on the table, so he did the same.

Once again he tried to concentrate on the board and decide on the next move. But his eyes kept wandering to hers. She winked at him. He winked back.

"Too bad." She reached over to put her hand on both buttons of the clock. Then took his five marks.

"What?"

"The time, it is over, yes? Five minutes each." She pointed to the clock face nearest to him. "Play you again?"

"Again?"

She pointed to her five marks on the table and he took five more from his wallet.

She reset the clock, and turned the board around so that this time she had the white pieces.

This time he shaded his eyes to stop himself from looking at her and concentrated on the game. He was weak at the openings, but had good instincts in middle game. With practice, he had become the best player in his barracks at Monterrey and at the language-listening school in Texas. He was not going to let himself be beaten by a woman, no matter how attractive she might be.

He moved quickly and slammed the clock. He'd make sure she didn't beat him on time again.

He took a piece, then another piece, then a rook, then her queen. He was proud of himself for decimating her position. Then she announced, "Mate."

He stared in disbelief. His king was well-protected, surrounded by pawns and pieces, with not an empty square around it. She had checked him with a knight and the king could not move out of check, because of all those defenders. It was "smother mate."

"So good you play." She set up the pieces again. "I was so lucky, yes?"

"Yes," he answered, in a tone of annoyance. He couldn't believe he had been so stupid as to miss that.

She pointed to her five marks on the table. He put ten marks on the table. She nodded in agreement and added five more.

This time Charlie attacked quickly with his queen, gobbling up stray pawns that she left unprotected. He could see no plan behind her moves. It looked as if she were trying to lose. Then his queen was trapped. All he could do was trade it for a knight or lose it outright. A few moves later, in a hopeless position, he resigned.

"Again?" he asked.

"Again," she affirmed.

He put 20 marks on the table and she matched it.

A few spectators started leaning over the table, and the waitress finally delivered the beef stew, but nothing could distract him from his game now. Charlie hunched over, gritted his teeth and moved his pieces with authority. They traded pieces quickly, and, a rook up, with two rooks and a bishop, he went after her king. He had her this time. He was sure of it. But she eluded mate again and again. Then she stopped the clock, announced, "Time," and once again took his money.

"Again?" she asked.

He didn't answer. He just put 50 marks on the table, and she matched it.

Now there were dozens of people gathered around, including the waitress, who once again held out her hand. "Zwanzig Marken, bitte. Fur das Essen."

Charlie paid her quickly, made his move and hit the clock.

Three moves later, he was mated. Scholar's mate. He had made one of the worst beginner's mistakes.

Someone laughed and muttered, "Was ein Grossmeister!"

Charlie took out his wallet, counted his money, set aside enough to pay his hotel bill, and put the rest on the table – 200 marks. She matched it.

This time he could make no progress at all. It was as if she knew his every move before he did. If she had been moving his pieces as well as hers, she probably couldn't have destroyed him more efficiently than she did.

"Gute Nacht," she nodded, and disappeared into the crowd with his money.

In July, Charlie returned to Munich. Once again, he set out in the direction of the English Garden, but this time his intent was different. In his satchel he had his 8 mm movie camera and a few books – Kafka's Castle in German, short stories by Gogol in Russian, and dictionaries. Max and Griff had told him that on warm sunny days, nudists gathered by the stream that ran through the middle of the park.

If the weather was bad, he would read. If good, he would enjoy the scenery and perhaps talk some young woman into posing.

As he crossed the Marienplatz, the sun broke through the clouds and the temperature rose quickly. It was still morning, and the park was almost empty. He settled down beneath a weeping willow beside the stream and started struggling through a story by Gogol, word by difficult word.

He fell asleep and woke abruptly when a drop of water hit his face. A group of young men and women, all naked, were playing in the stream near him. He pretended to read again, so as not to seem to stare. He was both embarrassed and fascinated. Fully clothed city-dwellers, business people on lunch break walked past on the path nearby, and naked sunbathers lay on both banks of the stream.

One young woman in a dark business suit stopped on the other side of the tree Charlie was leaning against. With her back toward him, oblivious to everyone around, she removed all of her clothing and stretched out on her belly on the grass.

Charlie put his book away. Not even in movies had he ever seen such a beautiful womanly shape. She lay just three feet away. He tried to think of something to say to get her attention and meet her; he tried to translate the words to German; but before he said a word, she was on her feet again, putting her clothes on as calmly and quickly as she had taken them off. Soon she was strolling away, probably back to the office.

Charlie scrambled to his feet, grabbed his satchel and followed her.

Her blond hair was shoulder length. Her brown leather pocketbook hung from a long strap from her left shoulder. She kept a tight grip on the top of it. The cut of her jacket and the skirt that descended to near ankle length obliterated any hint of the shape that had mesmerized him.

Seeing the gate toward which her decisive stride was taking her, he raced down a side path, out another gate and down the sidewalk toward her exit. There he pulled out his movie camera, braced himself against the stone wall and aimed in her direction.

She was still a hundred feet away. He zoomed in on her face and nearly dropped the camera.

It was the chess player.

As she strolled by, she looked him straight in the face, "Ach, mein Herr. Make you movies as good as you chess play?"

"No, I mean yes. I mean..." He tripped.

She laughed and walked on.

He caught up.

"Are you free tonight?" he asked.

"You mean you cannot pay?"

"I mean... Shit! You know very well what I mean."

———————

That night they met for supper at a little restaurant near the train station. Charlie made no pretense of understanding the menu. He let her do the ordering. Her name was Irene. She worked as an administrator at the University.

"And what do you with this camera of yours? Play you tourist? Or tell you stories with pictures?"

"I'd like to get into the movie business after my hitch is up. But I have a lot to learn."

"Indeed. Nimzovitch, did he about this write?"

"Seriously, I do have stories to tell in film."

"And I, too, stories have."

"Tell me a story," he coaxed her.

"So you can steal?"

"I'll trade you one for it."

She hesitated, took a sip of beer, then continued. "In the Bible, the crucifixion story, the soldiers make a man cross carry for Christ. Simon of Cyrene he is called, and saint for this holy act he became.

"Imagine that scene. Only this time the man they will crucify is not Christ. A false Messiah he is — not the Son of God. See you this with the camera inside your eye?

"The false Messiah a cross pulls. Many who believe in him watch. Through a big crowd walks he. The false Messiah stumbles and stops. The crowd closer comes. The soldiers their swords draw. The captain a man picks from the crowd and him to carry the cross makes. This man the false Messiah does not believe. But this suffering man, willingly he helps. Like you this?"

"But what is the story?"

"The story I told — the Messiah is false. Does that not questions for you make? Is this man less holy than Simon?"

"No, of course not," Charlie answered without thinking. He couldn't see that there was any issue at all. "Any unselfish act — even if for the wrong reason — can bring you closer to Him."

"I like your God." She took his hand and squeezed it.

"But what other answer could there be?"

"Many think God a puzzle maker is. If you the wrong Messiah follow, if you the Holy Grail miss, if you the wrong wish make, then must you wait at the door of the castle forever. Others believe no God there is. No God these puzzles make. Random and meaningless. So one little story can different ideas give, of God and of life. A good story that, nicht wahr?"

"But you could never make a movie out of that."

"Jawohl. Not me. But the next Bergman could make it."

"Who?"

"Ingmar Bergman — The Seventh Seal, Through a Glass Darkly..."

"I never heard of him."

"Mein Gott! And you movies make? What kind of movies make you, Herr Arnold?"

"I'm thinking of a scene. I'm not sure of the shape of the whole movie yet. But I like this scene. Imagine a young boy, maybe 16, running along a deserted beach. In the distance he sees a sunbather. He slows. It's a woman. As he walks closer, he sees that she is completely naked, lying on her belly. She is ten, maybe even twenty years older than him. She is beautiful. He has never before seen a mature woman naked in person before. He almost runs away. But her eyes are closed. She is sleeping. Slowly, quietly, he steps forward to get a better look.

"Suddenly, she rolls over on her back. But her eyes are still closed, and she puts a towel over them to block out the glare of the sun.

"He stares. It is as if he were reaching out with his eyes and caressing her entire body.

"He is standing right next to her. She smiles, and he realizes that she has been watching him from under the towel — she knows he's watching her, and wants him to watch her.

"He is petrified. She is more than just an object for him to fantasize over. She has her own wishes and ends. To her, he is just an object. She grabs hold of his ankle, and with her other hand reaches up as she sits up, and caresses the inner side of his thigh.

"He cringes for fear that she may be a mad woman. She may maim him. But he doesn't run. He stands still while she pulls down his bathing trunks, and pulls him on top of her and in her.

"When she is done with him, she gets up, puts on her clothes, and walks away, leaving him exhausted and bewildered in the sand."

"Persona, of course," said Irene.

"What?"

"Persona, the Bergman masterpiece. You who say you don't know Bergman have described a scene from his movie Persona. You a good eye have and a way with words. And you like a professional can lie."

Irene reached across the table and caressed his cheek. "Your God I like, and your dirty mind, too. Yes, you will good movies make. Yes, we will together good movies make."

———————

Charlie returned to Munich every weekend after that and stayed with Irene at her apartment in Schwabing. She was 24 – four years older than him. She had advanced degrees in both literature and mathematics and was a chess master.

That winter they planned the movie "The Pictures of Charlie's Wedding," and the following spring they filmed it. He never proposed. They simply hired a real minister to perform a real wedding ceremony as part of the movie.

They planned another far more ambitious movie as well – "Saint Smith," based on another story Irene told him.

CHAPTER EIGHT
THE OUTHOUSE

After Hank Arnold retired, he and Sarah fell into new and comfortable habits. They each had favorite parts of the house into which to retreat to be alone. He would go to the vegetable garden; to the workshop in the basement; to his study, with its floor-to-ceiling bookshelves; or to his rocking chair in the living room. She would settle with a book in the alcove by the fireplace, or on a window seat in their bedroom.

One Christmas, Russ and Fred bought them a television set with a 25-inch screen. But Hank and Sarah found they had no time to watch it. They would have liked to donate the set to charity, but kept it so as not to hurt their sons' feelings.

Hank would always find things that needed fixing, and work to be done in the yard and garden. Sarah would always find some corner of the house that needed to be cleaned or dusted. They both complained regularly about how big the house was and how difficult to keep up; but when Russ or Fred suggested that they move to an apartment, they both objected angrily. The house was too much a part of their lives for them to be separated from it.

It was more than just history that tied them to that structure. Hank had designed and built it when he was young and prone to experiment. The exterior was of stucco and stone, accented with wood at the corners and around the windows. The roof sloped this way, then that, in a multitude of angles. Overall, it had the look of a Black Forest cottage.

Hank and Sarah stayed in touch with their local community. They bowled together with the Senior Citizens Club, and read the paper together every morning. They were both active in the church; attending the Reverend Schumacher's services every Sunday, and then listening to Billy Graham and the Lutheran Hour on the radio.

Some of their children and grandchildren visited each Easter, Thanksgiving, and Christmas. But the first time in four years that the whole family came together was in July of 1966 at their Sixtieth Anniversary.

Russ and Rachel in Philadelphia had four children at that time: Frank had just finished his freshman year at Yale, Eddie was a sophomore in high school; Johnny was eight and Mark was just a few months old. Fred and Francine in Missouri had two sons, Jimmy and George. Charlie and Irene had been married for five years, but had no children.

Charlie and Irene arrived first; then Russ, Rachel and their boys. When Fred and Francine arrived, they all went to church together, where the Reverend Schumacher led Hank and Sarah through a re-enactment of their vows. Then they had a mid-day meal at the Gateway Restaurant. Fred had arranged it all for them.

After the family got back from the restaurant, Charlie brought out his new 16 mm movie camera. He had a new plot he wanted to try out, using family members as players. This time he was doing a movie called "The Out House", using the tool shed in the backyard as the main prop. He had everybody sit in lawn chairs and one by one get up and go into the tool shed, where he had painted a half-moon on the door to make it look like an outhouse. Since he was working without sound equipment, he could shout his directions as he filmed.

"Okay, Jimmy, you go in now. Nobody pay attention to him. Now, Jimmy, come out and do whatever you please. Just stay out of range of the camera.

"Okay, everybody, you're all reading the Sunday paper or talking to one another or looking off into space. That's right. Now, Irene, start looking itchy, like you've really got to go. Keep looking at the tool shed. Now go on over there. Knock on the door. Knock harder. Okay, you can't wait any longer. Open the door and go in.

"Dad, look up from your paper, like you're wondering what's going on. Eddie, you too, look like you're curious. Now, George you get up and go in."

One by one they all went into the tool shed. Of course, they came out again as soon as the camera was pointed away; but to the camera eye, they were all still in there.

Hank was the last one left. Looking curious, playing his part to the hilt, he got up and walked around the tool shed, scratching his head. Then he opened the door and stared in disbelief.

"That's where I'll splice in some footage of Fifth Avenue at rush hour," explained Charlie.

"Way out!" said Eddie.

"Way out?" muttered Rachel. She had been skeptical, but now she finally got the point. "Yes, it really is an 'Out House' then."

"Yes, the ending is good," Irene affirmed. "Much better than Bergman's spiders."

"Can we eat now?" asked Eddie.

"Go ahead, run on in," Rachel told him distractedly, looking over the scene again, as if she still didn't know if Charlie's effort was clever and artistic or simply a waste of everyone's time. "Will you add sound later?" she asked.

"The whole point is that it's silent," he insisted loudly. "I'm building on the limits of the medium. It's... Hell, if I could just say what I wanted to say, there wouldn't be much point in making a movie would there?"

CHAPTER NINE
THE LIGHT HOUSE

A couple of years later, the family assembled again. Sarah had been admitted to the hospital complaining of severe and persistent pain in her lower abdomen. After a series of tests, they realized that it wasn't indigestion or an ulcer or blockage of the colon, but rather the advanced stages of cancer. They had sent her home from the hospital as a hopeless case.

Charlie brought along his camera and lots of film, not because he was clinical and unfeeling about his mother's impending death, but rather because that was the only way he could try to understand and cope with it.

Afterwards, Charlie turned this experience and the interviews he conducted of his mother and relatives into his most ambitious film – "The Light House". It didn't bring him great fame and fortune, but he did win a prize for it at the Montreal Film Festival.

The loose structure of the film echoed Charlie's silent movie "The Out House". One by one, Charlie interviewed everyone just before they walked through a doorway into an unseen room.

The film included shots of Great-Uncle Harry, Hank, Fred, Rachel, Russ, Frank, and Irene.. It began with handheld shots Charlie took on the way there — roads, forests, traffic, and buildings racing by. The motion came to an abrupt halt at a closed door. Then Charlie spoke as narrator while the camera scanned the house, both outside and inside, upstairs and down.

"Sarah Brehm was born in 1892," said Charlie, "in Plymouth, New Hampshire, a small town, whose greatest claim to fame was that Daniel Webster lost his first court case there. She lived at 4 Russell St., just a block from the Pemigiwasett House, where Nathaniel Hawthorne had died and where she met her future husband.

"She was doing maid's work during summer vacation when she met Hank Arnold, her husband-to-be. He had come north for the mountain air, on his doctor's recommendation because of allergies.

"Aside from those allergies, Hank was muscular and tough. He was the eldest son of a Pennsylvania farmer and grandson of a cabinetmaker. Hank wasn't interested in farming. From the day when his grandfather first showed him how to make elaborate sand castles using boards for support, Hank dreamt of building real houses. After finishing high school, rather than become a farmer, he ran away from home and hiked to Washington, where the building trade was flourishing. There he got a job as a construction hand and eventually became a successful builder.

"The house he built for Sarah and himself was in part his vision and in part hers. Hers were the stone hearth, with its hearthside seats and niches and shelves, and in the bedrooms the window seats that opened up like storage trunks. His was the exterior with its mixture of stucco and stone. His, too, were the pear and apple trees, and the raspberry and blackberry bushes planted all around the house. Sarah would have preferred rose bushes, but Hank insisted, 'What's the point of a plant that doesn't bear fruit?'

"They had three sons – Fred, Frank, and Charlie – and a daughter, Sue, who died young."

The camera now scanned the living room, where the relatives had assembled.

"Charles Arnold, you turn that camera off this moment," bellowed Rachel, and the camera zoomed in on her angry face. "This is not the time or the place for that sort of nonsense. It shows a lack of respect for your mother."

"This is the devoted daughter-in-law," Charlie chimed in.

"How could you?" said Rachel, turning away.

"We must apologize to the audience," adds Charlie. "Rachel Arnold is the wife of Russell Arnold, second oldest son of the almost deceased."

Rachel turned and glared at the camera. "How can you speak of your mother that way? With the Lord's help, she will recover and live many more happy years."

"Rachel Arnold enjoys watching soap operas and denouncing the morals of the characters and of the actors and actresses who play the parts," noted Charlie.

"You're impossible," she tried, unsuccessfully to push away the camera.

"Right now she is tired, having been up for 48 hours, working hand-in-hand with her dearly beloved sister-in-law Irene Arnold, nursing the nearly deceased."

"How can the rest of you just let him do this?" Rachel exclaimed, looking around at everyone else.

"Charlie needs to do it," Frank offered. "Just let him be. It's his way of coping."

"Coping? You call that coping?" Rachel went on. "His mother is fighting a battle against death – and winning it, I believe, I sincerely believe, against all odds..."

"'Do not go gentle into that dark night,'" Charlie quoted. "'Old age should burn and rage at close of day.'"

"For that much you're right, Charlie," agreed Rachel, "Indeed, 'Rage, rage against the dying of the light.' All we can do is fight."

"Fight to the bitter end," added Charlie. "Fight despite all obstacles. Fight despite nature itself. 'And death shall have no dominion.'"

"Indeed," Rachel agreed again. "What more do we have than life? Nothing's so precious as life."

"There we have it, folks," commented Charlie, like a moderator on television, shifting to the tone he uses for commercials. "We have here the independent, unsolicited endorsement of an average housewife. Life, yes, folks, Life itself — the finest product on the market today."

"You're absolutely impossible!" Rachel shouted, threatening the camera with her fists.

"Now setting aside for a moment this marvelous product named Life, let's return to our topic for today, Mrs. Sarah Brehm Arnold. What do you think of the old lady?" asked Charlie, putting the microphone in front of Rachel's lips.

"What do you mean?" asked Rachel, disconcerted by the microphone, suddenly self-conscious.

"Let's be honest, now. She can't hear you. We're all family here. You were an orphan weren't you?"

"Yes, I suppose you could say that. Technically, yes. I was raised by my father's brother — my aunt and uncle, who now live in St. Louis."

"But you never spent much time with your mother-in-law, never spoke to her much, never showed any particular affection toward her."

"That's not fair of you to say, not fair of you to judge. We were close the first few months after I married Russ, when we lived here with her. I have many fond memories of that time – especially the time when she and I took you to your first movie, and later playing Monopoly with you and the Reverend Schumacher. Who are you to judge, anyway? I've always worked hard. Nobody ever got anywhere worth getting to without working hard to get there. It takes drive to get anywhere in this world. If I've done nothing else for my children, I hope I've given them drive."

"And what does that have to do with the nearly deceased?"

"I've always been busy. There's never been much time for idle chatter or indulging the emotions. I went my way, raising my family, just as she went hers. It wasn't like we lived right next-door to one another. There simply isn't time enough for everything and everyone. I intended to stay close to her, to be like a daughter to her. But never seemed to find time, except the occasional family gatherings, and then there was never time to really talk – we were always either preparing a meal or cleaning up after one. There was always something else that needed to be done for Russ, for the kids, and, yes, for myself. Next thing I knew, twenty years had passed, and now here she's nearly gone."

"So here you are slaving for her in her final hours, acting the part of a devoted and loving daughter."

"I'm not acting a part. I do love her. She's a marvelous person. She needs me, and I help – it's as simple as that. I only wish she were at a hospital where there are people who can do these things far better than I can. If it were up to me, she would be in a hospital."

"With needles and tubes coming out of her every which way?"

"If need be. Anything that might extend her life, just a little longer. As long as there's life, there's hope."

"And then what?"

"Why must you be so morbid?"

"Time for another commercial folks: Life – love it or leave it. Life Eternal. Life Everlasting."

"Will someone shut him up?" yelled Rachel.

"Maybe you better check on Mother again," suggested Russ, taking her by the shoulders and guiding her toward the door. She opened the bedroom door and went in.

Irene started to follow her, but Charlie grabbed her arm and pulled her back.

"Ah, yes," said Charlie. "Here we have the charming Irene Arnold. Alias Irene Heinz. Alias Iris Heinz. Alias Helga Heinz. Wanted in every state I happen to be in."

"Please to take that hand off me."

He released her, but she stayed in front of the camera.

"You, too, seem exceptionally devoted to the woman in the next room. Do you agree with your dear sister-in-law that the hospital is the best place for this patient?"

"Not at all, as you know, nicht wahr? Better that she die peacefully in her own home, among those who love her."

"Then, unlike your sister-in-law, you are convinced that she is dying?"

"Naturlich. The doctors say it's a matter, at most, of a few days. All they could do at a hospital is give her drugs, to put her to sleep so her last living would be no different from dying."

"With no pain?"

"Yes."

"And that would be wrong?"

"No. If that is what she wants. But she said she wants to see her house and her sons and husband. So I insisted that they let her come here. And I do all I can to ease her mind, to make her ready, to help her find strength and understanding within her to accept, with peace, the death that must come."

"A time to live and a time to die."

"So it is said."

"A stream flows into the ocean and becomes one with it and is no more."

"That, too, is true."

"God, heaven and hell are all within us."

"That I do not know. But strength and peace can be found within."

"You and your sister-in-law must make a fine pair – she raging for war against death and all of nature, and you preaching peace and acceptance."

"We get along fine, thank you. She cleans the sheets and the bed, and I clean the patient. She cooks the food and I serve it. There is too much to do to argue. We both love her and wish for her the best. Common ground that is."

"Perhaps the news that you are pregnant will give my mother joy in her final hours," suggested Charlie.

"No," she answered. "I will not lie to her I cannot. Let her leave loving the world as it is, not as it might have been."

"What do you mean?"

"Abortion," she whispered softly, so only he and the camera could hear.

"What do you mean?"

"I don't feel good about it," she admitted, still in a whisper. "But I did what I knew was right for me, personlich, as a person. My body is mine. No one, not even a husband, has the right to force a baby on me. For me, it was right. For you," she laughed, "you'll hate me for it. For the world, who knows? Was it another Einstein? So it was right, but not right – both yin and yang. Maybe the baby was right, but the time was wrong. Maybe now, as you would say, 'I owe the world one.'"

Charlie slapped her hard, while continuing to hold the camera steady.

She showed no sign of pain, and quickly left through the door to the bedroom.

Russ rushed up to register his objection, "How can you expect Irene to put up with you? – hitting her and in public, too. God, Charlie, when will you grow up?"

"Ah! it's big brother speaking. Welcome, big brother. Russell Arnold, renowned insurance executive."

"Actuary."

"Yes, indeed, an expert in the statistics of mortality. How apt, considering the circumstances."

"Get off your high horse," Russ pushed him back with a sweep of his hand. "You're nothing but a ham, and never have been. Give you a microphone and you act like you own the world."

"This is an historical narrative about a typical American family. Right now, we're focusing on the oldest son, who left college in a fit of patriotic ardor or academic failure to defend his country in World War II."

"You know very well that Fred and I wanted to join up, but couldn't pass the physical – me with my flat feet and Fred with his dislocated shoulder. Then Uncle Harry let us know that people who were in far worse shape than us had gotten in. Mom was furious when she found out.

"Uncle Harry had stirred up the dream of a military career even before the war, with his tales about Paris and Constantinople and Cairo; all his photos and picture postcards from World War I; the exotic coins and stamps he'd slip in our pockets whenever he saw us; and the books about war he gave us every Christmas and birthday. You'd think that war was the greatest thing that ever happened to a man – a chance to see the world and be a man among men. Personally, I didn't find the swamps of Georgia and Louisiana particularly delightful."

"You did, however, find the girl of your dreams."

"I did?" he paused, staring off at the ceiling as if remembering.

"Your wife, of course, the charming Rachel Arnold."

"Yes, of course, Rachel, yes, Rachel," he repeated absent-mindedly. Then he, too, went through the door.

"And here is Uncle Harry himself, the debonair war-monger," Charlie continued.

"What was that, sonny?" asked Harry, coming close and leaning an ear toward Charlie. Harry was 91 years old. He was once nearly six feet tall — very tall for his generation — but his back was now bent so badly that his head was no more than five feet above the ground.

"Had any more dreams, Uncle Harry? Any more war dreams to pass along to the kids? You know, you have to watch what you say, Uncle, because dreams are contagious. And Lord only knows what will happen once they get in someone else's head."

"You have to speak up, son."

"Harry! Harry! Harry! Step right up and see your niece."

"Knees? You say knees? No, nothing's wrong with my knees, thank you. My knees are fine."

One after the other, each family member entered the room where Sarah lay. No one came out. And the camera never looked in.

Hank appeared, sitting in a rocking chair, talking about old times with his grandfather at the beach. "Did you go by horse and buggy?" asked Charlie.

"No, not if we had a ways to go; and the Jersey beaches were quite a ways for us. We'd go by train. The trains went everywhere. From Lancaster to Philadelphia and from Philadelphia to Ocean City. It was quite an expedition, and I was lucky to have a grandfather who went in for things like that. And he did, believe me. He enjoyed it probably more than I did."

"Was he a good swimmer?" asked Charlie.

"He couldn't swim a stroke, as far as I know. That's not what the beach was for, you see. The beach was a place for castles and dreams, that's what grandfather loved."

"Sand castles?"

"Not just your ordinary run-of-the-mill sand castles. No, indeed. Grandfather could do anything with wood. He could take a stick that was six inches long and carve it into a chain of links that stretched to nearly a foot. And he used wood to make his sand castles."

"Driftwood?"

"No, he brought the wood along with him on the train – pieces he had carved to just the right size and shape for his plans, based on real castles in Europe."

"He must have attracted large crowds," Charlie commented.

"He didn't want crowds. He'd look for a stretch of beach where no one was around."

"Those castles must have been very sturdy, with all that wood to support them."

"No sturdier than most. The tide would wash them away, just like any other."

"You mean he didn't build them high on the beach, sheltered from the tide?"

"Of course not. What would be the point of that? He liked to watch the power of the sea. Sure, we'd retrieve the wood. That was my job. Then we'd build again for the next tide. We could always build a new one, as long as we had our dreams and our drawings. And when the time was right, the sea would come again to take it away. I always loved the sea."

Hank went into Sarah's room, and the door closed. Then the camera focused on the door,

From behind the camera came the sound of Sarah playing the piano, then Sarah's voice, reminiscing. This audio portion had been recorded a couple years before.

"'A mighty fortress is our God...'" she sang. "Come on, join in, Charles," she urged. "Surely, you know the words. You sang it in Sunday School. You always had such a deep voice for such a little boy. Surely, you haven't forgotten? It hasn't been that long. And the Bible. You must remember your Bible. Read a little every night. That will keep it fresh in your mind. 'A mighty fortress is our God...'" she began again, then stopped and laughed. "My mind wanders. It's blasphemous, I suppose; but who could blame an old woman for letting her mind wander. Age has its rights and privileges, you know. Like when I think of a fortress, I can't help but think of you and your father at the beach on the Potomac, building sand castles. Your father was always so careful about it, making drawings and gathering bits of wood and cardboard. And you'd just fill a bucket with sand and turn it over, building quick little ramshackle towers — so proud that you could make so many castles so fast. And when your father finally did build a beautiful and delicate castle, like the ones his grandfather had made before him, you'd jump on it and knock it to pieces before the sea could. You were a devilish little fellow, and still are.

"Russ and Fred were always so respectful when he built one of those castles, like it was something religious. And they'd try to protect it from the tide, though your father always built it close enough to the water so nothing could save it. And when they were little, when the tide ruined a castle, they'd get upset. But not you, my little gremlin. You'd make short work of your father's fortress.

"'A mighty fortress...' Yes, there are many fortresses and houses in the Bible. In my father's house there are many rooms. You've never seen my father's house, have you? I mean Grandpa Brehm's house up in New Hampshire. Of course, my Dad had passed away by the time you were born, and strangers had bought the house and were living there. But still I'd have wanted to show you. It's far bigger than this one your father built.

"Maybe someday, on your own, you'll go up there and look for it — 4 Russell Street, Plymouth, New Hampshire. I'm sure it's still standing — maybe with a different color paint, and maybe they've turned part of the barn into a garage.

"It was one of those double kinds of houses — where the barn and the house were joined, so you didn't have to go out into the snow to get to your horse and buggy. There were only a few rooms with steam heat, that you could use in the winter; but in the summer, you could play in these huge attic rooms, and the barn and the loft of the barn, with a cupola on top; and even what we kids called a 'secret passage' — the crawlspace under the peak of the roof that led from the barn to the attic.

"I'd dearly love to go back to that house myself, and crawl through that passage once again. I've dreamed of it so often through the years that I'm not sure what was and what wasn't there. In my dreams there's this secret room, where I stored my most precious things — things that have been lost for years: a rusty iron ring a boy gave me in grammar school, a notebook of poems I wrote, and photos of Sam, my brother who ran away from home. Only sometimes it's not just their pictures that are there, but they themselves, and Sue, also, my daughter Sue. They've just been playing a game of hide and seek. I just had to find the right room."

Now the door opened, but instead of the sick room, with Granny in bed, a street sign appeared — Russell Street — and another door with the number 4. Then that door opened and half a dozen kids ran out.

Sarah exited very quietly a month and a half later, after most of the family had returned to jobs and school. Irene was sitting in the bedroom with her, reading a paperback collection of movie scripts. It was her turn to watch in case Sarah needed anything. She didn't notice the moment of passing. She thought Sarah was still sleeping. An hour or two later, Hank came in to give her pain-killing pills and found her stiffening form.

The Reverend Schumacher conducted the funeral service. "I knew Sarah for thirty years," he explained. "Over that time I've gotten a reputation for the eccentric interpretations I give to biblical passages in my sermons. I must confess that Sarah was my inspiration. She had a wonderful and naive faith in the power of language – of all languages. At Christmas she'd wish us all 'Mary Christmas, and Joseph New Year.' She was intrigued by the echoes she'd hear – the meanings and associations that appeared as if by accident of translation. She felt they were part and parcel of the mystery of God, and we would puzzle and rejoice over them together.

"When her daughter Sue died, we puzzled over the passage: 'There are many mansions in my father's house.' I liked to think of the word 'mansion' in the Latin sense of stages of a journey – the notion that this life is just one stage in a much longer journey. Sarah preferred the English sense of 'mansion' as a huge house with many rooms, and dying as moving from one room to another or one mansion to another. I imagine her now, a little girl, standing in a vast and strange new mansion – lost and in awe; not frightened, just very curious, as she has always been.

"Today, in pondering what to say as a farewell, a hackneyed phrase came to mind: 'And now Sarah is with God.' I had a moment of recognition – an epiphany, like an electric shock. It was a typically 'Sarah phrase.' Just a few months ago, she had puzzled over the echoes of "Mary was with child," and "the Word was with God". And now I cannot help but think, 'Sarah was with child, and now she is with God.' And may the mystery of those words be revealed to her in everlasting joy."

THE CHOICE

He was in a long winding corridor of a hospital-like building. The man beside him, who was acting as his guide, kept referring to him as "my lord". That felt good and comforting. But there was something about this place that reminded him of a nightmare.

"It must be a recurring nightmare," he explained to his guide, "because I remember it so vividly. It was so real – the blazing heat, the smell of fresh sweat layered on weeks of unwashed filth, the pain so sharp, like nails pounded through flesh."

"And that reminded you of here, my lord?"

"In my dream, I was given a choice. I could be born into that world where life was brutal and short, where I would die in nail-sharp pain. Or I could live in another age and another place."

"Well it's hard to imagine a time and place better than this, my lord. Here life is sweet. There are billions of people in the world and many find a vocation that suits their talents and their interests – work that they can take pride in. And through their combined efforts, all benefit from an abundance of goods and pleasures."

"My memory must be failing me. What you say rings true, but it sounds new to me. I feel disoriented. I feel uncertain of things I should know as well as my name. This world feels less real to me than that other one I dreamt of. In that world most people died by 40 of accident or war or disease. But I've forgotten — what is the average life span here and now?"

"Over eighty, my lord. Healthcare has eliminated many diseases that used to be fatal. And our world is far safer and more peaceful than that other horrid place and time you dreamt of."

"And forgive me for asking — it must be the aftermath of that dream, the shock, the pain in my feet and hands: this real world around us pales in contrast — what do people do with that life time? How do they spend their golden years?"

"It's interesting that you should ask that, my lord, in this very place."

"What is this place?"

"It's a home for the elderly, my lord."

"A special home for them? They don't live in their own homes or with their families?"

"Here they get special care, my lord. Their meals are made for them, and all the tedious chores of life are taken care of for them. They benefit from controlled diet and exercise and the very best geriatric healthcare — to extend their lives even more. And trained staff are ready to take care of any contingency twenty-four hours a day, seven days a week."

"But what do they do for themselves? What do they do with their time?"

"They watch television. They play bingo and scrabble and solitaire. Some read."

"I imagine with their advanced age, their bodies must be frail. They must be limited in what they can do."

"Indeed, my lord. many are confined to wheel chairs."

"Like this one?"

"Indeed, my lord."

"It's so nice of you to take me for a stroll like this while I recover from the pain in my feet and hands, the aftermath of that terrible dream. And you are so kind and patient to explain all this to me — what I should know as well as my name."

"It's no problem at all, my lord. It's always a delight to talk with you."

"And these people, these elderly in this happy happy world we live in, while their bodies may be weak and their activities limited, they have their memories to enjoy over and over again, right? That's the reward of a long virtuous life — to remember all the good times and the good friends — am I right?"

"Yes, my lord, more or less."

"And where does this long winding corridor end?"

"What, my lord?"

"That door we're headed to — all the others we've come to have been double doors that swung open as we approached. But that one is a single door with a handle. And as we get closer now, I see there's a keypad next to it, like a telephone keypad. Yes, my memory is getting clearer now. I remember telephones, now, with touchtone keypads."

"Excellent, my lord, you'll be back to yourself in no time."

"But what's beyond that door? I don't remember."

"Don't trouble yourself about that, my lord. No need to trouble yourself about anything. We'll be in there in a moment. I just need to enter the code."

"The code? You mean that's some kind of a lock?"

"Exactly, my lord. You are your old self again."

"Then this is..."

"The Alzheimer's Wing, my lord."

"And I live here?"

"Yes, my lord."

"And I have no memory?"

"It comes and goes, my lord. On a good day, you can remember my name, and your own, as well, my lord."

"But this is a mistake, a terrible mistake. I fell and hurt my feet and hands. I'm in rehab until they get better and I can get out of this wheelchair and go home to... to ... Where did you say I live?"

"You live here, my lord."

"But this is a mistake. I didn't choose this life."

"None of us does, my lord. None of us has a choice."

"But I did. I did have a choice. I was special. I was chosen. I was the son of God."

"We are all God's children, my lord."

"But it was real. The sun was blazing. I was coughing with dust in my throat. I would have done anything for a taste of water. Then I was lying on my back on the ground. My arms and legs were tied to boards. They drove nails through my hands and feet. And when they raised the cross and planted it in the ground, my weight pulled me down, tearing my flesh against the nails. The pain. The pain. And I begged for water. The thirst was almost worse than the nails."

"Here's some cold apple juice, my lord. That should make you feel better."

"But there's been a mistake. Take me back! Take me back! Nail me to the cross! Please, God, nail me to the cross instead!"

THE GENTLE INQUISITOR

Estaban had always been a zealous Dominican, wishing to do all he could for the good of the order and the glory of God. He had been in monasteries since the age of ten, and he loved the life: the tranquility, the libraries with their theological treasures, the tradition of so many lives over so many centuries devoted to the service of Christ. At an early age he had been ordained as a priest and had become a professor at the theological academy in Seville.

But he felt that it was selfish of him to spend his life so quietly and securely feeling the presence of God about him. His students had all taken their vows, had given their lives to Christ; but outside the academy walls, millions of people rarely thought of Christ or thought wrongly of Him. He had read of such people time and again. And many of his former classmates were directly confronting such people, taking an active part in the Inquisition. So Estaban requested that he too might take part in that great work of saving souls from perdition.

That was how it came to pass that one day a young priest found himself as the chief prosecutor in the case of a young Jewess who had paid lip service to Christ while continuing in the abominable ways of her ancestors. The highest dignitaries of the church were assembled with all the official robes and insignia of a great religious festival. He tried to restrain himself from the sin of pride, to remember that he was acting in the service of God, that what mattered was not his own eloquence, (which surely was superfluous since she was known to be guilty), but the soul of the young Jewess who must be forced to confess and must be burnt at a great and glorious Auto de Fe that she might, with the grace of God, be granted everlasting life. And so many others like her needed saving: a great new career in service to God was opening for him.

But he found himself saying things he never expected to say, found himself, in fact, pleading in her behalf in front of the entire Court of the Inquisition. It was quite embarrassing, a shocking display. And to make matters worse, he spoke well, too well, much better than he had ever spoken before. It was unfortunate. She was acquitted, and ever after that he had her soul on his conscience. All his prayers and penance did nothing to erase his guilt: his action was unthinkable.

He apologized again and again to his superiors and friends; and they could tell that he was sincerely penitent. They tried to comfort him, assured him that he meant well and that in the eyes of God that was what mattered. They would see to it that he would never again be placed in such a difficult situation. He was evidently unsuited for the pressures of courtroom oratory. Another task would be found for him so he might work for the good of the order and the glory of God.

But, unfortunately, the young Jewess, through his folly, had never been brought to a true understanding of her sins, had not been humbled to repentance, in fact still considered herself innocent, had no fear for her soul; and was grateful, immensely grateful to Father Estaban for saving her from the flames. And her family was grateful (though they were now much more careful about their public behavior). And her friends were grateful (though in public they dared not let it be known that they were friends). And Estaban kept receiving, even months after the trial, anonymous gifts and tokens and letters from well-wishers. The gifts he donated to the order. The tokens and letters he destroyed, trying to erase that scandalous incident from his mind.

His superiors wanted him to return to his old professorship, but Estaban requested that he be given a task, however humble, that involved the saving of souls. So Estaban became the confessor of several of the greatest nobles of Seville. And at first the job delighted him: having contact with real people and real problems, being entrusted with the care of souls that were in daily danger. But then it struck him how trivial were the sins that were confessed to him: mere matters of lust and avarice, pride and ambition. And he became more and more deeply convinced that he was a greater sinner than any of them, having lost the soul of the poor young girl. Who was he to absolve anyone of anything? It was more likely that his advice would corrupt rather than cleanse the moral lives of these fine upstanding people. Estaban requested to be relieved of his duties, to be given some still humbler task of saving souls, one befitting such a sinner as he.

And so Estaban became a seller of indulgences. And he was a fine salesman, eloquent about the miseries of hell and purgatory, adept in his argumentation, in the way he summoned evidence in support of the effectiveness of indulgences. And though his superiors were disappointed that such a fine young scholar insisted on taking up such a lowly task, they were pleased with the results, for many hundreds of souls were advanced in the celestial hierarchy toward lesser misery and much fine marble could be bought for St. Peter's in Rome and the glory of God.

But it soon came to light that Father Estaban had on occasion given indulgences to beggars. It would have passed unnoticed, for he paid for them out of his own pocket: but it so happened that one of the beggars took offense, was quite loud in his complaints that he asks for bread and this priest gives him a fancy piece of paper that promises in Latin that after he's dead he won't have to suffer quite so many years.

It created a scandal: giving indulgences to beggars. Why in no time everyone would be expecting the Church to just give them away. Why It was contrary to the whole spirit of the thing. And Estaban recognized his error, did penance for having been so weak, for having forgotten that pity is one of the most powerful weapons in Satan's arsenal.

In his guilt and despair, Father Estaban returned to his books, buried himself in the abstruse studies of his youth; and it was in such studies that he discovered his true calling.

He felt drawn to heresies, to their intricacies and subtleties. It was amazing how rational and convincing some of them were, how subtle the ways of Satan. It would be easy for anyone, even he Father Estaban to be seduced into taking the false for the true, the Anti-Christ for Christ.

Of course, in retrospect, the scholars of the Church always untangled the true from the false, pointing out the source of the error. But to be confronted with a new heresy, one that was not yet officially recognized, that had not yet undergone analysis: that would be frighteningly difficult for a learned priest to properly understand, much less the ordinary lay believer. And time and again throughout history, hundreds, thousands, perhaps even millions of souls were lost, damned for all eternity before the Holy Catholic Church had time to diagnose the disease and begin its curative efforts.

It occurred to Estaban that if heresies could be described and analyzed before they captured people's imaginations, many millions of souls could be saved. And the logic of heresies, the reasonableness that made them so convincing, made it possible for someone well versed in theology to imagine the ramifications of shifts of emphasis, of slight changes in the True Doctrine as they were developed and expanded. He dreamed of compiling a compendium of all possible heresies, conveniently indexed, so that even the simplest carpenter could check his idle musings and be assured that he had not unwittingly fallen into deadly error.

The Grand Inquisitor did not like the idea. But he gave his approval nonetheless, so this zealous priest could have a harmless task to content himself with, a task that might after all prove useful.

So Father Estaban set about his work. And he was amazed at how easy it was to imagine new heresies. In just a few years, he composed over 7000 heresies.

The slightest change in wording or in interpretation of a word could lead to mortal sin. For instance, in the opening sentence of the Gospel of John, the standard interpretation rendered the preposition "pros" as "with." But in classical Greek it was quite possible for "pros" plus the accusative to mean "against." On the basis of such a slight change one could claim that "In the beginning was Reason and Reason was against God and Reason was God." In other words, Reason by its very nature is opposed to God but, in fact, is itself God Himself. Variations on those opening passages of John alone gave rise to 253 heresies. And there would have been still more if Estaban hadn't grown weary of the theme.

He loved best the heresies that dealt with Christ incarnate as man, with his man-ness and his god-ness and their varying degrees and interrelations. That was the most difficult point of theology:

how God could be man. And a simple carpenter. It was hard to connect the abstruse formulations of theologians with the life of a simple carpenter. But to fail to do so was heresy, a heresy that every carpenter since the time of Christ had probably fallen into, had probably only avoided by never asking the question.

And Christ himself, the carpenter — could he have known that he was God? Of course, all is possible to God, but God-as-man? How far a man?

Perhaps he was even man enough not to know all these subtleties. Perhaps he considered the behavior of his disciples extraordinary. He was amazed at his own behavior in front of crowds, saying things that he never intended to say. This interpretation would clear up some of the apparent contradictions in the gospels. Sometimes he spoke as God and sometimes as a man who, as far as he knew, was just a man, unambitious, finding it difficult to explain his own behavior and to restrain the reactions of his friends.

And he had been among us twice: both before and after the Resurrection. And if he didn't know that he was God the first time, perhaps he didn't know the second. And one day waking up in a stone cold tomb, enshrouded and anointed like a corpse, he frantically unbound himself, trying all the while to convince himself that this was a nightmare, though he found it difficult to remember the other world he lived in when he was truly awake. He stumbled as he walked out into the bright Easter sun, so painful to his unaccustomed eyes. Two women who saw him screamed and ran away. He didn't mean to frighten them, or the soldiers either. But that was the way with dreams — sudden shifts of scene, transformations, and people forever over-reacting.

Everything he saw was probably symbolic of something he wanted — the holes in the hands and feet probably indicated that he was nailed down to some job, some pattern of life that he found deadening and wished to break away from at all costs, in order to start a new life in a new place among new friends.

All these people and places struck him as unfamiliar. He kept hoping it would end soon. And it did. But from beginning to end, it was an extraordinary dream in which he was forever surprising himself with his own behavior.

And, reasoned Estaban, if Christ had been among us twice unbeknownst to himself and had on those occasions announced at inspired moments that he would return again, then perhaps he had returned, perhaps many times, but had passed unrecognized. Perhaps he is even now among us.

Father Estaban broke out in a cold sweat as he reread his pages. They were in a sense "inspired." He had let the words and ideas carry him whither they would. They struck him as unfamiliar as he reread them now. "Exceptionally good," he told himself near the start. "A veritable gem," he told himself as he neared the end. "It alone will make my compendium a work of art." He tried to restrain himself from the sin of pride.

But now he remembered the last sentence, and he was afraid to read it. He dared not turn that last page, dared not see the sin of sins committed so clearly in his own hand. He painfully remembered the incident with the Jewess, tried to excuse the present circumstance as another case of that madness. But, fortunately, this time it was only his own soul that was at stake. No one had yet read the words. Not even he had read those words of his madness, not his words, even though he had written them. No, he wasn't the author. And no one would ever read them.

He pulled himself together, took several deep breaths, then calmly and quietly gathered up his manuscript and calmly and quietly burned it in the same hearth where he had burned the tokens and letters from friends and relatives of the Jewess. But as the last page went up in flame, a doubt arose in his mind. He was no longer certain that the words on that page read, 'I am the Christ, the son of God.' He was no longer sure, and it disturbed him profoundly that it might not have been so.

As he wandered through the streets of Seville in despair, he was disturbed that he was disturbed. He needed to speak to someone, but he dared not turn to his fellow Dominicans, for how could they sympathize with a priest who wanted to be Christ, who wanted not just to be like Christ, but to be Christ in the flesh – to forever do the "right" without necessarily even thinking of God.

Yet he didn't know and couldn't believe that that was in fact what he wanted. It was just an illusion. He had never written it. And afterwards he was distraught, not in command of his senses, having just destroyed in a matter of minutes his life's work. And he couldn't tell the Jewess or her family either, as they welcomed him with great rejoicing and spread a feast before him.

And so it came to pass that Father Estaban no longer worked for the good of the order and the glory of God, that, instead, he learned the trade of a carpenter and lived a simple, long, and quiet life.

CREATION STORY

"What are you laughing at?" Adam smashed the stone, the meticulously polished stone, so carefully carved, reproducing every detail of the face and body of its proud fashioner.

He had been amazed at his own handiwork, and had for a day and a night sat before it, staring, touching himself and then the statue, then himself — especially the lower lip, which he had finished last and of which, in his first surge of creative joy, he was most proud.

It had been the boulder to the sunset side of his fire. He had been just Adam-the-cave-dweller, just Adam-the-wielder-of-clubs. He had been alone and without purpose.

At first he had chipped away idly. He chipped to hear the sound of stone on stone, to hear any sound that was not of the forest, the fire, and the wind. He was tired of listening to the garbled, fading echo of his own shouts. Stone on stone was sharp, precise; and soon he could see that the boulder was not the same as it had been before he chose it: the pattern of even his random chippings was unlike the wear of wind and rain. He was changing his world. This stone was his. This stone was him.

In his first excitement, as he began to see the crude outlines of a possible man, a possible self-likeness in the stone, he rushed and hacked, and in a passion pounded.

On the third day from that first vision, the stone cracked — from projected head to projected hip and across both thighs. Cracks must have been in the rock before he began. He had not noticed. They must have been aggravated by his persistent pounding. He had not noticed.

In despair and exhaustion, Adam collapsed by the broken stone.

He must have dreamt in that sleep of exhaustion. For when he awoke, he was calm. He knew now that the statue would be small, smaller than the smallest uncracked section of the boulder; that it would be an exact likeness of himself; that he would proceed very carefully, not from any fear that he was unequal to the task, that he could blunder, but rather because he knew that this was his project, the source of his hopes and joys, that, in the process of creation, the statue would absorb all his energy, all his thought, all that he would call "Adam."

He would proceed slowly and savor the effort of creation.

And so he did. Until he stopped.

For a day, he sat and gobbled grapes and ripped the warm flesh from a freshly roasted antelope and laughed and patted his belly in the noonday sun, proud of his handiwork, proud that he, Adam, not just lived in the world, but shaped it with his hand. The world was his, for he would leave his image in it, in this stone that already had the oblong shape of a man, the outlines of arms and legs, a hint of fingers.

Adam even fancied that, on the left hand, the index fingernail was broken just as he had broken his, accidentally, while chipping away at that very hand the day before. He was so pleased with that touch that he was hesitant to tamper with it.

And the strokes that suggested his wild fuzzy hair: it was so difficult to create the illusion of hair in stone. He had done it by luck, not skill or plan, and yet it was right, even in its present crude form. He doubted that he could make that stroke if he tried.

And the beginnings of feet. He could swear he even saw his protruding vein over the left ankle of the left foot. Incredible good fortune.

It was as if the statue were making itself, as if he, or rather his image, were already in the stone, and the chips were falling away of their own accord; or, rather, he was acting as the instrument of some unknown force.

He laughed uneasily. Who was he? What was he trying to do?

Adam looked at the stone, and it was as if he looked at it for he first time. He didn't know what to do with it. He didn't understand why he had spent so much energy on it, why he let it sit on that soft, cool spot where he himself used to sleep so comfortably.

He reached for the statue. It was strange to his touch. No longer was he an "artist." Once again, his hands were the clumsy hands of Adam-wielder-of-clubs.

He pushed the stone aside and went to sleep.

———————

Weeks later, when at noon he was again gobbling grapes and warm antelope flesh, Adam noticed the stone by a pile of other stones he had kicked when frustrated by unsuccessful hunts. He lifted it, brushed off the dust, and smiled at his former folly.

This "statue" had raised him to such a passion. It was so crude.

His "work of art" was barely distinguishable from a stone worn to the shape of a faceless, featureless man by the chance workings of wind and weather.

But there were strong lines to it. It had been cut with the grain of the rock, and the long lines of that grain from head to toe now absorbed his attention.

It was indeed a fine stone he had chosen. And Adam could imagine it carved in the shape of a man, perhaps even a self-image.

With the first stroke, the first microfine chip, the old fervor returned. He chipped again. This time he knew he must not stop except to sleep and eat, must not contemplate his handiwork until it was complete. And he must proceed slowly that it not be too soon finished.

But his persistent labor carried him onward despite himself, until he had given shape to the final lip.

It was done. It sat there and stared at Adam. It stared dumbly, blankly, lifelessly. And for a day and a night, Adam sat in front of it — proud.

He smiled when he realized that the stone not only had his features, but was grinning, too, just as he was grinning: one a reflection of the other.

He pouted and stroked his limp lower lip, pulled it still further down, making grotesquely comic faces.

His own lip felt so strange, so foreign, so inert — just another form of matter. It was more pliable than stone; but like stone, it was just raw material for a fashioning hand to work with. But whose hand?

He had no more made himself than the statue had made itself. But he was alone — alone with his creation and without a creator.

He had freed this stone from the grip of chance, had enabled it to shed these useless chips and become what it could become — this created shape.

But what of he himself? What could he become if he were freed from the raw material of himself?

"What are you laughing at?" Adam shouted at the stone.

And he smashed the stone, the meticulously polished stone, so carefully carved — smashed it on the broken remains of the boulder of which it was once a part.

Legs, torso, the head, and one arm fell on the soft ground where Adam often slept. And in the evening shadows, they seemed to be parts of several Adam-statues, sprouting from the ground.

CHIANG TI TALES

The Void

(written December 1963)

Long, long ago, before man made books to talk across centuries, a young man, Chiang Ti, left his village in the valley and went up to the mountains. With all the comings and goings in the village, no one had time to think beyond the next harvest. But Chiang needed to know why the sun rose, and why the grass grew, and why men lived and grew and died. So he went up to the mountains, close to the sky and the stars and the sun.

After a few weeks in the mountains, Chiang Ti went running back to the village in the valley and gathered his parents and his neighbors, all the important people of the village and all the ordinary people too, like the young girl Lotus and her sister Little Blossom. He told them all, "Every child has this answer in his drawings. The sky is above; the earth is below; and man dwells in the empty space between. Life is the journey of the soul from heaven to earth through this emptiness.

"A child knows of heaven for he has recently come from there. A dead man becomes a part of the earth. Therefore, let the knowledge of a man determine his tasks. Have babies serve as priests and old weaklings as kings. The babies will teach you the language of the gods. And the old will teach you the value of life and the futility of greed and will pursue a policy of peace."

Many of the village folk were impressed with Chiang's words and were willing to do as he said. But the oldest man present asked, "If what you say is true, then you, Chiang, are not yet halfway in your journey through the emptiness that separates heaven from earth. How then could you, far from both heaven and earth, have discovered the key to the universe?"

Chiang Ti paused a moment, then turned and slowly climbed back up to the mountains, to think once again about the problems of the universe.

Metamorphosis

(written April 1965)

Months later, Chiang Ti returned again to the village, with a smile of certainty on his face, his round bright head held high. Lotus saw him first and called together all the village folk.

He told them, "What is done is done. Man has no control over his past. He changes and learns. He is not the same person today he was yesterday; and tomorrow, too, he will be different. Life is a process of becoming. You cannot relive the past and alter it. But you can control what you are becoming. Judge men not on their past, but on their future.

"A keen observer can see what a man is becoming. A man can begin to look like a frog or act like a pig. Bit by bit he can become more like an animal or vegetable until when he dies, his reincarnation, his change of bodies makes but a small difference.

"From the beginnings of life, some animals have become better, others have stayed the same, and others have fallen. Be ruled and guided by those who are rising; and under their good influence all might rise together. Be not corrupted by tomorrow's zoo. A monkey who acts like a human is better than a man who acts like an ape. Judge all by what they are becoming and be ruled by the best."

"Who then will be judge?" asked someone in the crowd.

"Me," said the Mayor.

"Me," said the Schoolmaster.

"Me! Me! Me!" arose from all sides.

As the villagers bickered, waving their arms and tongues, Little Blossom tossed breadcrumbs to pigeons that swarmed about, flapping their wings and pecking greedily. Chiang Ti watched the villagers and the birds for a while, then turned and slowly walked back toward the mountains.

Never-ending Now

(written April 1965)

The following spring, Chiang Ti returned again to the village with a new answer. "A human life has no beginning and no end," he said. "The time of the sun and the stars is not the time of man. His mind has a time of its own.

"An hour's sleep is but a moment. And the second before a race begins can seem to last for hours. Imagine a condemned man on the scaffold with the rope around his neck. To him, how long does that moment last? What thoughts run through his mind? One minute to live, half a minute, a quarter, an eighth... And what minute, half minute, quarter, eighth... did you begin to be? The promise of eternal life was in the endless moment of conception. It's fulfillment is in the endless moment of death.

"What need is there for laws, judges, prisons? The final judgment, hell, and paradise are within you. Just remind people of the horrors or pleasures that could await them in that last endless moment, and there will be no more crime. All will live in peace and love."

But the doctor said, "Many people die in their sleep, unaware that death is approaching. Does your theory apply in that case? Or do those people simply die – with no heaven and no hell?"

Chiang Ti suffered a century of frustration. A moment later, he turned and walked back to the mountains to look within himself for other answers.

Peace

(written August 1965)

Chiang Ti watched in horror as each spring a large band of strong young men crossed the mountains to the neighboring valley and as each fall a few came limping back. He had heard the gossip and speeches of how the war began and why it continued. But he knew that the whys of a war are like the whys of a thunderstorm or an earthquake: they help to predict, but do nothing to prevent or to stop it. Long did he meditate in his mountain hermitage on the problem of making a lasting peace. Then in his moment of greatest despair, when he feared there was no answer, that very fear gave him the answer.

That night he descended to the village in the valley; secretly, for this was not an answer for the ears of the many. He went first to the home of Chow Wong the politician, for he was a man of action.

"Rejoice, Chow Wong, the answer has come. War will soon leave our village and the village in the neighboring valley. Fear in part drove us to war. Fear will also save us. For fear is a great unifying force. If a common enemy were to challenge both villages, our petty differences would soon be forgotten for fear that we'd lose the more pressing struggle. And likewise, fear could unite three, four, a dozen, any number of villages if it were great enough and pressing enough. Of course, with a real enemy, nothing is gained: more blood is shed; and as soon as the great struggle is over, the petty differences are remembered, and the old war flares up again. But if the enemy should be an imaginary one from beyond the stars or beyond the Great Sea, surely then the fear could last, with all men cooperating to prepare for the imminent invasion.

"Others have tried this before, shouting with foaming mouths that the end of the world is at hand; so that all men should act like brothers. Such men failed because they had no authority beyond their own frenzy, no credentials other than their own claims of divine inspiration. We shall succeed because we shall speak through the mouths of those they already trust. We shall win to our side the handful of daring mean who have crossed the Great Sea or the handful of learned men who know the ways of the stars; and with all the weight of their indisputable authority, we shall spread the alarm through all the land. Lend me your hand, and together we shall chase war beyond the farthest sea."

Chow Wong replied, "I fear that fear that you would use so lightly. If all went well, if most, nearly all believed the story and the panic took constructive form, all might pull together to work for their common safety. Villages might cooperate, at first. But bit by bit, the pace would quicken; for the danger must seem to grow or people will get used to it and no longer fear it. At first all would need to be prodded to be convinced that the danger was getting greater. Then events would start to flow of their own accord.

"The hundreds of separate village governments would be too inefficient to direct this life-or-death struggle with the unknown. A single government would take the place of the many, and a single man would take charge of that. Meanwhile, a few would not believe and would loudly voice their views on street corners. In such an emergency, no mercy would be shown. Dissenters contribute nothing to the cause and hamper the efficiency of others: hence they should be destroyed. The greater the fear, the greater the unity necessary to combat the enemy. Hence, bit by bit, the useless fringes would be eliminated: the old, the sick, the weak. Everyone is expected to produce to the maximum. The lazy would be destroyed. And as the enemy is expected at any moment, the pace would become greater; more and more wouldn't be able to keep up, and they too would be destroyed. Fewer and fewer would remain to work harder and harder until the ultimate unity: one man alone, facing the universe.

"And if you should see the rock of humanity careening down the mountainside and place yourself in its path to stop it, you, too, would be destroyed. No one would believe you when you told them it was all a hoax. You'd be destroyed with the rest of those too weak or too lazy to continue.

"No, Chiang Ti, fear is not the answer for peace."

Chiang Ti returned to his hermitage in the mountains. And in his fear of war and its consequences, in his fear that there is no formula for eternal peace, Chiang Ti felt very much alone: one man facing the universe.

Creation/Destruction
(written April 1966)

Night followed day, time and again. Rocks tossed high in the sky fell low in the valley. Chiang Ti watched and pondered, then rose and returned to the village in the valley, followed by Lotus, Little Blossom and dozens of children who loved to hear his stories.

"Whatever rises must fall," he told the village folk. "Whatever lives must die. Every creation contains the seeds of its destruction. But don't despair that it is so. Rather, accept and rejoice in the rhythm of the world.

"See a child at play with his blocks, carefully, cheerfully building. See the delight of creation. Then see the same child, with a sweep of his hand, topple the tower, laugh, and build again.

"To create, one must destroy; and to destroy, one must create. The whole pattern has its pleasure – both rise and fall. Accept it cheerfully, like a child, and continually rejoice."

But a carpenter, accustomed only to building, spoke up, "Chiang Ti, your very idea is a creation. So if every creation contains the seeds of its destruction, then your idea too must be destroyed."

Chiang Ti smiled, turned, and took the path back to the mountains. Slowly he climbed, pausing now and again to toss pebbles.

Lotus
(written June 1967)

So once again Chiang Ti returned to the mountains. But this time Lotus followed him. While he sat staring at the horizon, she went up to him and asked, "What are you doing, Chiang?"

"Building my world," he replied.

"What are you building it with?"

"The mountains and the sky. But I'm not yet sure whether the mountains are hanging suspended from the sky or if instead the sky is but a roof supported by the mountain peaks."

"What will you do when you know?"

"Then I'll build the foothills and the forests and the village in the valley."

"But the village is already there. I just came from the village. Houses still line the streets. The fountain still flows by the marketplace. Children still play. I'm sure the village is there."

"Yes, but I hope to firmly establish the village in knowledge. To see, to feel, to touch is not to know. Knowledge is like a house. Before you can build the rooms that people live in, first you must clear the ground and build the foundation."

Lotus smiled, for now Chiang seemed to be speaking a language she understood. "Wang Li-wu is building a new house on the far side of the winding river," she said. "He and my father go there every night to clear the ground and talk about how beautiful the new house will be. And Sung Fu-lan has said, too, he will help when construction begins. It's a lovely spot – just at the base of the far mountain. Is this where you plan to build your new house? This too is a lovely spot; and if I were going to build here, I too would not return to the valley for many days, but would sleep here in the cave, as you do, and spend my days deciding where and how to build my house. When you are ready, I will come to help you; and father and Wang Li-wu will come also."

"Thank you, Lotus; but you do not understand. I am not building a house. I am building a world, and the house is just a symbol."

"My father, too, speaks of symbols. Each evening when he goes to help Wang, he says he is going to the new world. And sometimes when our house needs a new door or the roof leaks, he says it's time to repair our world. And sometimes when I or my brother has scraped a knee, he says, too, our world has hurt itself; and he washes the wound gently. And he says that someday soon I will have to build a world of my own together with my future husband, and he hopes the world will be at peace and be a good world to live in. Who then is the girl you are about to marry?"

"You do not understand. I am not about to marry any girl. I came here to the mountains to think in solitude; so I might build my world. The village in the valley is too distracting. There one never sees the sun climb over the mountains or the stars spread from horizon to horizon. In the evening here, a nightingale sings of the beauty of the mountains."

"Yes, Chiang, father says everything has its season, that one shouldn't sow grain in mid-winter. And he says that one day I will feel a restlessness in me, and the world of my father will no longer be my world, and I will have no world, but will want a world of my own; and I will wander with the wind looking for my world, and all thoughts will be brilliant, and all men handsome; and the sunrise will be my sunrise; and the nightingales will sing for me only; and even the grass will tell of the pains and joys of growing."

"Yes, Lotus. But still you do not understand."

"Let us sit by the old acacia, Chiang. There you can explain to me why the mountains must hang from the sky or the sky be supported by mountains. I love to hear you talk about the mountains and the sky and why things are the way they are. You think so deeply for one still young. I could never begin to know why things are the way they are. But please explain. It's so fun to hear you talk and to try to understand. And there by the old acacia, we can listen to the grass growing, and at evening hear the nightingale, and in the morning watch the sunrise together."

Blossom
(written June 1967)

So Lotus went often to the mountains with Chiang. And Chiang often returned to the valley with her. Being with her was a joy, and telling his thoughts to her brought greater satisfaction than telling the entire village. Often he treasured her responses, for she had a way of completing his thoughts and making them tangible and immediate.

For her, he chose his words carefully, "All things spontaneously being themselves: the sunrise, the nightingale, the gnarled acacia; each thing so separately itself, unfolding with its own particular subtlety, coyly curved upon its stalk a lotus blossoming..."

"There are many flowers in the garden in front of our house," Lotus replied. "Each morning mother carefully waters them. At evening their fragrance fills the house."

"... It is in its separateness that each thing reveals its own beauty," Chiang continued. "All things differing from each other, it is in their very difference, in being themselves, always unfolding, changing, but each in its own particular way that all things participate in the beauty of the sunrise, of the nightingale's song. The lotus rejoices in being a lotus, the way it bends with the wind and rises to meet the sun, and rejoices too in the way the wind rushes to bend it and the way the sun watches and waits, patiently..."

"Lotus, sunflower, morning-glory, snapdragon... Each morning mother waters the garden," explained Lotus. "Little Blossom follows her with a pitcher and at each plant as they pour, mother states its name, and Little Blossom repeats its name and sometimes I hear her telling each flower its name, teaching them as mother teachers her: lotus, sunflower, morning-glory, snapdragon..."

So they came to live in happiness together in the valley. Chiang no longer needed the mountains. He saw the world through the eyes of Lotus; and Lotus, without seeming to try, found the world everywhere.

The World
(written June 1969)

Then one day, Lotus left without a word. This time it was she who had gone to the mountains.

Chiang found her by the old acacia. "Your father said you were restless, that you wandered alone in the mountains, and I knew it would be here by the old cave and acacia I would find you. But why wander alone?" asked Chiang. "You know, I too could come here to listen to the nightingale, and we could together watch the grass grow, and talk of building..."

Lotus interrupted, her eyes scanning the horizon, "Our valley is very small. Are there many houses in the next valley? Is there a carpenter, a butcher, a schoolteacher? Are there many young girls like me and young dreamers like you? What do people talk about? What do they do? Surely there must be more to do than walk about the barren rocks day after day; more to look forward to than a house like everybody else's house, with perhaps a few more flowers, and a houseful of children to grow up and someday walk these same, barren rocks. Surely, it must all lead somewhere. There must be change and growth, even if it's the gnarled twisted growth of an acacia. Even if here it is winter, somewhere it must be spring. Surely, Chiang, the world is big enough to always have a spring. Surely, somewhere nature must be bursting with life so that the ground trembles as the grass grows and the birds sing. Chiang, how big is the world?"

"I too once found our valley small and wandered over the mountains," admitted Chiang. "But the next valley is like this one and the one beyond is but the same."

"That's a story you must tell me someday," said Lotus. "I like so much to hear your stories."

"But I already told you."

"Odd. Well, someday you must tell me again. But for now, I need to be alone, to find my own way in the maze of thoughts."

THE MIRROR

A middle-aged man in a business suit is about to walk out of his apartment. He reaches toward the doorknob, then halts abruptly. There is panic on his face. He tries again and again, but he can't bring himself to touch the doorknob.

He checks his pockets, his hair, his shoelaces, making sure everything is in order. Something is wrong. He doesn't know what, but he simply can't leave the room until he figures it out.

He turns around and starts checking and straightening everything in sight. But still something is wrong, something he can't identify.

Finally he turns toward the mirror over his bureau. Once again he checks pockets, hair, shoelaces. He checks his wallet, his zipper, his tie.

Once again, he halts abruptly. He feels the tie at his collar. Looking down, he sees the tie hanging in front of his shirt. But the image of himself in the mirror has no tie.

His eyes open wide as he looks from mirror to tie to mirror. It's a dull green tie, held in place by a silver-plated tie clasp. It goes well with his gray suit. But it simply doesn't appear in the mirror.

In the mirror, he himself looks the same as always. His height and build are the same. He'd recognize his face anywhere.

Everything in the mirror is the same as everything he sees on him and around him — the gray suit, the white shirt, the black shoes. Yes, that's certainly his own face, with an expression of confusion and fear.

He shuts his eyes, turns around and looks again. Still the image in the mirror is not wearing a tie.

He goes to his bed and lies down again. Then he gets up and walks to the mirror — still no tie.

He undresses, climbs back into bed, gets out of bed again and dresses again, just as before. Then he walks to the mirror — still no tie.

He tests the image in the mirror as if it might not be real. He moves a hand quickly, then both hands, and the head, and the hips, and a leg — faster, and faster. The image in the mirror falls at the very same time he falls.

He gets up, smooths out his clothes, clenches and unclenches his fists several times.

Then he checks his watch, takes a deep breath, and stares again at his image in the mirror.

Finally, he takes his tie off, hangs it with his other ties in the closet, calmly walks to the door, turns the doorknob, and enters the world.

THE BARRACKS

Building 3926, Fort Polk, Louisiana, was a "temporary" structure – a white clapboard oblong rectangle, hurriedly thrown together, like hundreds of other army barracks. Its first tenants were recruits and draftees bound for the Pacific in World War II. Cycle after cycle were trained and shipped. Then the war ended, and the barracks fell silent, except for the bats that nested under the eaves, like ghosts returning to curse drill sergeants who had not pushed them hard enough, and not taught them what could have kept them alive.

Later, when a "temporary" war broke out in Viet Nam, the "temporary" barracks was reopened. Exterminators were called in to eliminate the bats, but while individuals could be killed, their kind was indestructible. At dawn and at sunset, their eerie forms hovered high above the eaves, and vanished one by one into the depths of the building.

Aside from the bats, the barracks was now in better shape than when it was first built. Cycle after cycle of trainees had kept it in shape for inspections. Some had even made improvements to get bonus points. For instance, there was a red rack for the red helmet-liner that the fire guard wore each night. Two magazine racks hung on the latrine wall beside the toilets. And on the wall above the water fountain, hung a home-made plaque that one group of trainees had presented to the drill sergeant they reviled and respected.

Downstairs, between two long rows of parallel bunks, was the masterpiece of the barracks – the red linoleum center aisle. Thanks to the special efforts of cycle after cycle of trainees, it shone mirror-bright. No other barracks in Echo Company could hope to match it. As long as they continued to take care of it and didn't get gigs for foolish oversights, the third platoon would always win inspections. That was a source of pride and confidence – feelings that were hard to come by in basic training.

Everyone in the platoon took their boots off at the door, but even in stocking feet no one in the platoon crossed the yellow lines that defined the center aisle – nobody but the chosen few entrusted with taking care of it.

In this cycle of trainees, Evans did the buffing upstairs. The all-important downstairs floor was in the keeping of Powell. Tagliatti helped him with the buffer cord. Schneider tended the plug.

At first it had been a continual annoyance having to walk all the way around to get to a bunk that was just three feet away across the aisle. But by now it was second nature. If anyone forgot, there was always somebody else around to shout a reminder and preserve the sanctity of the center aisle.

The screen door slammed, and Beaulieu, a tall, tired National Guard trainee from the University of Maryland, shuffled in. The latrine lay to his right, the staircase straight ahead, and the downstairs bunkroom stretched out far to his left.

"Where's Roberts?" he shouted across the bunks, shuffling his stocking feet lazily as he walked in.

"How should I know?" shouted Hathaway from the far end. A football-playing college boy from Alabama, he was stretched out on his belly on a top bunk, writing letters.

"You're his squad leader, aren't you?"

"Yeah, but not his nursemaid."

"He's got CQ from four to six."

"Big deal."

"Somebody's got to take it. Shit'll hit the fan if only one guy's on CQ."

"If you're so goddamned uptight about it, do it yourself. You can't go anywhere anyway."

Hathaway kept writing.

Beaulieu turned, stepped toward the door.

"Keep your goddamned feet off that center aisle," shouted Hathaway, without looking up from his letter.

Beaulieu stopped short of the yellow line, kicked a footlocker, turned, and shuffled behind the bunks.

"Pick up your feet," shouted Hathaway.

He stopped, then continued to shuffle. The screen door slammed again.

"Goddamned trouble-maker," mumbled Hathaway.

"He's only trying to do right," offered Schneider, a fat farm boy from Iowa, in the next bunk.

"No, I mean Roberts. Why the hell'd they ever put draftees in this company? And why did they have to stick us with them?"

"You know damned well — they were recycled."

"Yeah, four fucking fuck-offs, and we got all of them."

Hathaway kept writing.

Schneider lifted his huge bulk, carefully lowered it to the floor, then waddled quietly behind the bunks, past the stairs and into the latrine. Straight ahead were the platoon's two washing machines, with dozens of bags of laundry lined up waiting their turn. Beside them stretched a row of sinks, leading to the showers. Along the other walls were urinals and a line of toilets, about two feet apart, without partitions. All but one toilet was occupied, like seats in the reading room at a college library just before exam time. Although everybody had his pants down to justify his presence in these plush accommodations, most were reading books, newspapers, or magazines, or writing letters home.

Roberts, a tall thin black boy from Mississippi, was standing by a sink, staring at himself in the mirror as he carefully shaved the top of his head.

"Hey, Roberts, aren't you supposed to be on CQ?"

"May be."

"Well, what are you doing then?"

"Giving myself a haircut. Got to look pretty for the sergeant."

Roberts kept shaving his head.

"Well, they're looking for you, Roberts. Don't say I didn't tell you."

"Yeah, everybody's looking for the old Bob tonight. I got me a date. Got me a couple of them. I'm going to have me a big night."

"You're going to have big trouble is all, if you don't hightail it over to CQ."

Schneider lowered himself onto the only empty john, between Tagliatti and Waslewski. "Hey, Tag," he asked, "are you through with the sports?"

"Yeah, but it's four days old."

"Well, that's two days better than anything I've seen."

Alec, a short, tough ex-cop from Chicago, entered the latrine. "Ah, shit."

"Yeah, Alec," said Cohen, a college kid from Berkeley "It's a full house. Maybe you can catch the next show."

"Bunch of damned exhibitionists. Got to spend the whole day with your pants down, in full view of the world."

"A good craps's one of the few pleasures allowed us," replied Cohen.

"Then shit and get done with it. This place looks like a fucking library."

"I say, sir, are the libraries like this in Chicago?"

"Get off it, Cohen."

"When I'm done, I will, indeed, get off it. But right now that's premature. I might risk staining this immaculate concrete, the pride of the third platoon latrine crew."

"Cut the bull."

"Me Big Chief Shitting Bull."

"Tag," said Schneider, "can you toss me the toilet paper, please?" He caught it, circus-style, on his big toe. He used some, then tossed the roll to Alec and stood up. "Here you go, Alec; it's all yours."

"Just shit right down and write yourself a letter," mocked Cohen.

"Formation!" the shout from outside echoed and reechoed throughout the barracks.

"Ah, shit," groaned Alec.

"No, my boy, self-control," Cohen kept ribbing him. "That's the first lesson of the Army. Self-control. Potty-training 101. It's all part of basic training. We must learn to adapt to the shituation."

"Well, you don't seem to have learned it — with that goddamned diarrhea of the mouth."

All five platoons of Echo Company lined up quickly on the exercise field. There were forty-seven men in the third platoon. Forty-three were National Guard and Reservists — all white. Four were draftees — all black — Roberts, Armstrong, and two new guys, recently recycled, that nobody knew by name.

143

In the summer of 1970, the Viet Nam War was being scaled down. Fort Polk, which had been, as the big welcoming sign still announced, "Birthplace of combat infantrymen for Viet Nam," was starting to train National Guardsmen instead. This was the summer after the Cambodian Invasion and Kent State.

These trainees came from all over the country and from all walks of life. They were given uniform clothes and uniform poverty. Their uniform haircuts seemed to wipe out age differences. It was like an experiment in elemental democracy.

They were a surprisingly well-educated group. Several had been to grad school. Most had some college. Most of the rest intended to go to college as soon as this was over.

There were no trouble-makers in the group. No National Guardsman or Reservist would want to get into trouble. They just wanted to get out of the Army as quickly as possible; and, if nothing out of the ordinary happened, they'd all be out, after basic and AIT or MOS training, in two to four months.

An artificial hierarchy had been imposed on this realm of social equality. The drill sergeant picked a platoon leader, an assistant platoon leader, and four squad leaders. It seemed he deliberately chose a pompous, overweight coward as platoon leader, to teach the trainees to obey someone just because of rank, not because of personal respect. This way they'd be learning to follow the system, to obey any stranger with rank, rather than a specific individual.

But the group was so small that they knew each other too well for artificial distinctions to matter. When the drill sergeant was around and when they were with the rest of the company, they observed the forms. But in the barracks, the platoon leader, Rawlings, was a joke, an outcast, the victim of repeated practical jokes, a convenient symbol of hated authority that could be mocked and mildly abused with impunity.

MacFarland, the assistant platoon leader, was exempted from fire guard, KP, etc. He had no responsibilities, and did nothing.

Hathaway, the leader of the first squad, was the real leader of the platoon. Vassavion, Sullivan, and Powell were bigger than he was, but ordering people came naturally to Hathaway. When something needed to be done, he took it upon himself to make the decisions that had to be made. Without debate or hesitation, he simply gave orders, and he was obeyed or evaded, but never overtly disobeyed.

Sanderson and little Evans always backed Hathaway, without his ever having to ask for help.

Powell was an exception to every rule. Nobody in the platoon ever told him what to do. And he never ordered anyone else around, unless they asked for his advice, as they sometimes did, even Hathaway, when the barracks was a mess and they had little time to get it in shape for inspection.

At formation, the Captain of Echo Company presided as the drill sergeants read their rosters and checked off the names quickly and mechanically. At the name "Roberts," several voices sounded off "CQ," and one voice said "KP."

The sergeant moved on to the next name without a pause. The roll completed, most raced to the mess hall to line up and wait for dinner.

A few went back to the barracks.

Frank Arnold and Alec headed straight to the latrine. Tagliatti, Waslewski, MacFarland, and Delaney stretched out on their bunks.

Halfway down the aisle, Powell sat on his bed, his powerful frame bowed, a Bible on his lap.

Waslewski spat out, "Goddamn piss-assed shit-hole. They treat prisoners of war better than this. I'd like to shove that Bill-of-Rights crap right up that mother-fucking drill sergeant's ass."

"That's the system for you," explained Delaney. "Here we are, supposedly free citizens, and they've revoked our civil rights and subjected us to this torture without there ever having been a declaration of war, without the express consent of Congress."

"All I want's a goddamn beer. It's piss-assed hot, and there's a PX a block away."

"Have a drink of water," suggested MacFarland.

"Water?" asked Waslewski. "You call that piss 'water?' All I want's a goddamned beer. Is that too much to ask?"

"Okay, Waz, okay. We're all in the same boat. You don't have to remind us."

"I don't see how that Sanderson does it," said Tag, "running laps in this heat."

"He's nuts," concluded Waslewski.

"He thrives on this shit."

"That's what I said: he's nuts."

"Good thing that Dietz can't count," noted MacFarland. "It sounded funny three guys on CQ."

"And somebody claimed Roberts was on KP, too."

"Where the hell is Roberts?" asked Delaney.

Waslewski licked his lips, "Maybe he just slipped over to the PX for a beer."

"Yeah," said Tag, "if nobody sees him, it'll be all right."

"Don't anybody tell Rawlings," added MacFarland. "That bastard would turn him in."

"Here comes Rawlings."

Everybody left in a hurry — everybody but Powell.

Rawlings laughed, weakly. "They sure got hungry fast."

Powell smiled.

Rawlings turned to the water fountain, took a swallow, and spit it out with disgust.

146

"The water ought to cool off while everybody's at supper," Powell replied, "It needs a rest. We all need a rest."

Rawlings skipped supper. For him, the rare quiet was well worth the price of hunger.

Powell stayed too, reading the Bible – at peace in his own world.

Twenty minutes later, Vassavion came staggering into the latrine, leaning on Waslewski. He had the flabbiness of a natural athlete who had given up exercise in favor of beer and repose. "At great personal risk," he announced to himself in the mirror, "and exercising considerable self-restraint, I have brought you a six-pack – six bright, sparkling, lukewarm, unopened, certified virgin cans of Schlitz."

Waslewski grabbed a can. "Drink up, my boy, drink up,"

Vassavion continued. "I feel the thirst coming on me. Man lives not by bread alone. Give me one of those cans. Booze and broads – it takes taste, refinement, and years of education to properly wallow in such shit. You must be a connoisseur, a kind of sewer. They have fine sewers in this city, full of certified grade-A, government-inspected shit. The whole world is shit. But few are those with taste refined enough to enjoy it, to savor the taste, the odor, the warm moist feel of it. Shit."

He threw down his half-empty can. "It tastes like shit. Luke-warm diarrhetic shit." He stumbled to one of the empty johns and vomited. "I do believe my constipation is over. Now I can even shit through my mouth."

Waslewski opened the last can. "You lucky bastard. I'd give my right ball to get out of this place."

Tag entered with his four-day-old newspaper. "Where's Evans?"

"Evans?" asked Vassavion. "He was with me a minute ago. While I was painting the town, he was looking for paint. The man has the soul of an artist."

147

Rawlings joined them in the latrine and nearly tripped over a beer can.

Vassavion greeted him magnificently, "Welcome, Prince Hal."

"You're drunk."

"Then be ye crowned king already? A hollow crown and an empty noodle. 'Tis true 'tis pity, and pity 'tis 'tis you."

"You're drunk," stated Rawlings.

"Amen. And hallowed be thy name. And hollowed be thy head. Howl, howl, howl, the beer is foul. A foul ball. We had a ball, and the beer was foul. Out of line, your highness, most definitely out of line. But I'll go straight from honest to goodness. Just don't 'arry me, me boy; I'll do it at me own speed."

"Please stay out of sight," Rawlings requested patiently while pissing at the urinal. Then he quickly buttoned up his fatigues and left.

Vassavion shook his head. "I do believe the old boy's pissed off. He has no sense of humor, no sense at all."

As Rawlings quietly climbed the stairs, Delaney, Armstrong, Alec, and Cohen stormed in and gathered by the water fountain.

"Okay, Armstrong, where's Roberts?" asked Delaney. "You're his bunkmate. You should know."

"Said he was going home."

"Home? Is something wrong at home? Somebody sick or something? He should have told somebody. They'd call the Red Cross and have them check it out. If it was really bad, they'd give him a pass."

"Nobody's sick. He said nothing about being sick. Just said he was going home."

"Freedom," said Alec. "You talk about freedom, Delaney. There's your fucking freedom. He wants to go, so he goes. And what can they do to him? Send him to Nam? He's fucking eleven bang-bang. Fucking mortars. He's going to Nam all right. No place but Nam. There's your fucking freedom – being so low you've got nothing to lose."

"That's fucking profound, Alec." Cohen started to sing softly, "Freedom's just another word for nothing left to lose..."

"Is he coming back?" asked Delaney. "Did he say he was coming back?"

"He'll be back," said Armstrong. "When he's good and ready, he'll be back."

"He's got thirty days," offered Alec. "I heard a hold-over talking about it. One of the ones waiting for court-martial. Thirty days and you're still AWOL. But one minute more, and you're a deserter, and they'll have the FBI after you."

"Fuck the FBI," said Delaney. "These days there are so many deserters the FBI can't hope to touch them. But when the drill sergeant finds out that Roberts is gone, he'll have the whole lot of us low-crawling from one end of the company area to the other. And we can forget about ever getting PX privileges or passes. Shit. I can't take five more weeks of this fucking hell-hole."

"You're not going to rat on him, are you, Delaney?"

"Hell, no. What's to gain by ratting on him? As soon as they know he's AWOL, we've had it. But if we can cover it up till he gets back, we'll be all right."

"That little bastard."

"How long do you figure he'll be, Armstrong?"

"Don't know. But Jackson, Mississippi's a long ways from here. And he don't have no money."

"Shit almighty."

Frank walked past, pulled his notebook out from under his pillow, and went to the latrine. "Delaney is a self-centered ass," Frank wrote. "He talks about principles, but he has none himself.

149

What he says is unrelated to what he does. If he thought he could get anything out of it, he wouldn't hesitate to turn Roberts in. But what bugs me most is that he wouldn't bother to rationalize it. He'd just do it and keep making the same speeches about freedom and human rights.

"When I first got here, I thought I'd found moral simplicity. The world was reduced to just this barracks and the barren sandy ground around it. We were all confronted with simple rules and orders: you obey or disobey; you cross the line or you don't; you are forced to act – to submit or rebel – in full knowledge of the consequences. The setup was artificial, but it resembled a scientific experiment – take away all class distinctions; and, in a limited, controlled environment, examine human nature. But there's nothing natural about Delaney – his words and his acts simply don't match."

Frank heard the door slam and stocking feet slowly shuffle toward the bunkroom. He didn't look up. He knew it was his bunkmate Beaulieu. He half expected to hear Hathaway hollering at him for dragging his feet. But Hathaway was still at supper.

Beaulieu got pen and paper from his locker and shuffled off to the latrine where he sat on a john across from Frank and continued a multi-page letter to his wife Debbie: "I just got off CQ. It's a bit early, but Sullivan can cover for me, say I'm at supper. Damn that Roberts. He'd never cover for me, you can be damn sure. But I had to cover for him or we'd all have been screwed. That's the way they work things here: everybody gets punished for what one guy does.

"But Roberts doesn't give a damn. With no sweat at all, he got perfect scores in all the PT events but the mile. The mile he did in ten minutes, jogging and walking beside Schneider. Poor Schneider was huffing and struggling every inch of the way, his heavy lard bouncing up and down and nearly throwing him off balance. And there was Roberts taking his jolly good time, laughing and joking.

The drill sergeant blew his top; put Roberts on night KP for a week. I'm sure he didn't go. He just doesn't give a damn, the bastard.

"I'm still sore all over. I never thought I'd live through it. We had those damned plague shots the day before, and I could have sworn I couldn't move my arm or swallow any food. But the bastards had us out there doing another PT test and laughed at our moans and groans; wouldn't let anybody go on sick call, the bastards. Needless to say, I didn't do well. And they'll probably have me doing extra PT all week because of it.

"Damn those bars. I can do the bars. Enough of them, at least. If you give me half a chance. But that first time, they took us to a field where the rusty bars spun freely so you couldn't get a grip on them, and they ripped your hands apart. Mine had just healed by yesterday, and then they got ripped open again on another stinking set of bars. Nobody could do them right, not even the guys who show off back at the company area. Nobody, that is, but that bastard Roberts and that runt Evans.

"Everything's topsy-turvy here. It's the big guys who are hurting, guys like Hathaway, Sullivan, and Vassavion — the football player types. Waslewski, too. They're strong all right, but they've got a lot of weight to lift, and they have to struggle to pass that damned test. And, of course, the fat ones, like Schneider, take a beating.

"It's the little guys that have it easy. That runt Evans got a 490 on the PT test. Just missed a little on the grenade throw and the rifle, or his score would have been perfect. It doesn't take any muscle to squeeze a trigger.

"So Evans came out tops. He and Vassavion. Evans with ease and Vassavion in agony. They got the first two passes. They just got back. Late. Little Evans was leading the lumbering Vassavion. We covered for them. It's hard to get mad at them. Vassavion is magnificent in his drunkenness. I've never seen him in better spirits. And Evans was lucky to have gotten him back so close to on time.

"That Evans is like a monkey the way he swings through those bars. Delaney nearly exploded when he heard the runt was getting a pass. I forget what he said exactly, but somehow it was an example of the injustice of the system, the topsy-turnviness of rewarding the weak and tearing down the strong. However he put it, it hit home — how they're breaking us in mind and body, reducing us to a general anonymous mass of weaklings. And something about runts being in collusion with them, being taken in and used. He says that's how the system perpetuates itself — putting runts and cowards in positions of authority, people who know damned well that their authority comes to them not for any merit of their own, but just because of the system.

"Listening to Delaney, I found myself hating little Evans and Rawlings, too. Rawlings isn't a runt. On the contrary, he's just as big and has just as much trouble at PT as Waslewski and Sullivan. I guess I lump Rawlings together with Evans because he's so self-effacing, so meek and retiring that you never notice his size. You naturally think of him as a weakling or a coward.

"I've got nothing personal against Evans or Rawlings, but the frustration and anger and hurt and sleeplessness all build up. And all the groveling in the dirt. You've got to let it out sometimes. It's easy to focus all that hate on somebody, almost at random, to take it out on him. And Delaney has such a way with words.

"I'm glad Hathaway was around then. Hathaway treats Evans like a kid brother, joshes him, knocks him around a bit, and looks out for him. I'm glad Hathaway was there then, or I might have taken a not-so-friendly poke at the kid.

"Here comes Sanderson. He takes it all in stride, as if this were pre-season football training, or as if all his life he'd wanted to break the five-minute mile in combat boots. When they pack a hundred of us into a school bus or cattle truck and we're all groaning, Sanderson coaxes Cohen to start up a song, and he sings with all his heart and lungs. And, God, Sanderson has quite a set of heart and lungs from all that running.

"It's a crazy world, Deb, that makes such crazy places as this, reducing men to chunks of sweating, aching flesh. Even trying to shit hurts. If you were here, or, rather, if you were near and I could see you, sleep with you, it would be tolerable. With you, I could tolerate almost anything. We could just lie here and laugh about it. This shit should never be taken seriously. It's just one huge practical joke. I'm sure that's the way the drill sergeants take it – like a fraternity initiation. Cohen manages to see it that way too, manages to bring out the humor in things.

"But it's degrading. The only way to release all this pressure, aside from taking a poke at somebody (which would land you with an Article Fifteen or a court martial and get you recycled and stuck in this damned army another month or two) is to masturbate. There's just no other way, and it's so damned degrading. In a barracks full of guys, the bunks no more than three feet apart, the firelight on all the time, the fireguard pacing back and forth, and somebody else in the upper bunk getting shaken by your every move. And you try to do it as unobtrusively as possible – one hell of a way to get a release, lying there stock-still, squeezing yourself with a sheet; but it works, after a fashion.

"My imagination takes charge, and I'm far, far from here, this place never existed, and I'm holding you so warm and close. Damn it, I'm horny as hell, and it'll be at least three months before I see you again. You can't imagine what this place does to a guy. I think of you constantly, whenever we get a five minute break, and I can lean against a tree and shut my eyes (they won't let us stretch out, ever), or even running laps around the block at 5 AM, before breakfast, and the thought of you gets me away from this place, and it's something to look forward to — the next moment when I'll be able to let my mind drift to you.

"Or maybe it's the body that does the remembering. Our minds have been reduced to pulp by no sleep, maybe four hours at most. (As Delaney points out, a soldier is entitled to eight hours of sleep. But the drill sergeants always cover for themselves. Officially it's always eight hours from lights-out to lights-on. Officially, it's our own doing if we don't get enough sleep. But there's always a half dozen chores that still need to be done after lights-out. And then they wake you up for fire guard duty or CQ; and then you have to break the rules again, getting up an hour before lights-on to clean the barracks or we'd never make it through inspection).

Without sleep, the mind loses the power to control what it's thinking, to tie thoughts together by anything more than simple association. It becomes a passive inert mass.

"It's the body that does the remembering. My muscles stop aching as they remember your shape, the pressure of you close to me, the texture of your skin, the delightful, unexpected ways you move. My eye muscles relive with my hands the fullness of your breasts. I remember directly, completely, not like before, the electric touch of your fingers, the playful flip of your tongue, the way you toss back your head to toss back your hair, your buttocks as you climb the stairs ahead of me (that's why it's always ladies first — so men can watch them move), your long legs rubbing softly against mine.

"Damn it. I want you. I ache for you. These aches have nothing to do with ten-mile hikes and PT and lying prone in the dust and the 90-degree sun for endless hours. No, it's my every muscle longing to be with you, straining to break away from these stupid bones and rush home to you. These bones are so stupid. This mind is so stupid. This nation is so stupid for having invented such a thing as basic training. How could anybody or anything ever sanction anything that might keep me away from you? My body can't understand. But here I sit and shit and write you endless letters.

"My bunkmate, Frank, is on the john here across from me. There are no partitions. He's writing too. Maybe it's a letter. He doesn't talk much to me. Hangs around with that Delaney character. But I know he probably feels the same as I do. I can feel the bed shake at night. That's not nightmares. We're all reduced to a common denominator.

"It may be that in the real world this Frank is an intelligent guy, but here he spends his every free moment sitting on the john, shitting and writing. I guess it's diarrhea of the mind. Everything here seems to get diarrhea on Sunday. That's the only time we can afford the luxury.

"I slept till noon, shat till two, had CQ till four, filled in for that damned Roberts till 5:40, and now I'm shitting again. It's been a luxurious day of self-indulgence. But in about two and a half hours the lights will go out, even though it's still light outside. And we'll all toddle obediently to bed. And it'll all begin again.

"Damn it. I need you. My body needs you. The pulp that was my mind needs you. Hell.

"You know how I always bitch to you and get it out of my system, then I forget it as we laugh together. It's great the way you make me realize what a fool I am for bitching all the time. You'd hate me the way I am now. I hate myself the way I am now. I can't even write you a decent letter. All I do is write about the shit around me. But damn it, darling, I'm caught up in this shit. All those stupid rules they threw at us five weeks ago are now a part of me. I take this nonsense seriously. My joys, fears, hopes, and miseries all stem from this world they've thrown me in. Somehow Sanderson and maybe Powell (I don't know much about Powell) have managed to keep living in their own worlds. But my world has been torn down.

"My body remembers your every move vividly. but it's hard for me to imagine the world we used to live in. It's all unreal and far away. The only world I've got is this shit. And I hate this shit. And I hate myself for letting myself be reduced to this.

"Damn it. I love you and miss you, and I'm sorry this is the way I write and the way I think, but they've done it to me, damn it. They've reduced me to this. When I get back it'll be different, and I'll be different. And I'll be able to forget all this and go back to being me — whoever that was. But wherever I am and whoever I am, I love you."

Waslewski tumbled into the latrine, picked up the empty beer cans, poured the few remaining drops down his throat, then absent-mindedly crushed the cans in his hand, as if they were paper cups.

"Evans, would you believe that Evans?" he bellowed for the benefit of Beaulieu, Sanderson, and Frank Arnold. "Never so much as tasted a beer. A weekend pass. Thirty-two hours of freedom. That runt had thirty-two hours in the land of bars and brothels, and he spent it chasing after paint so he can pretty up the barracks. What a waste."

Beaulieu looked up from his letter. "Paint?"

"Yeah. And that ain't the half of it. You know what color he got?"

"What?"

"Yellow."

"What the hell can he paint yellow?"

"The lines. The fucking lines for the center aisle. Those fucking lines we're not supposed to step over. He wants to repaint them

156

so they'll be nice and neat and pretty. He thinks it'll be worth bonus points for inspection. Bonus points. God, that runt's out of his ever-fucking mind."

Waslewski tripped on a laundry bag, then sat down on it and stretched out on the long line of laundry bags, swallowing the last drop of the last can with a cherubic grin on his face.

The screen door slammed and Alec walked into the bunkroom.

"Take your damned boots off," hollered Hathaway.

"Don't be a pain in the ass," whined Alec. "It's Sunday. Cool it."

"I don't give a damn if it's Doomsday. Take off those fucking boots."

"Go ahead, Alec," Schneider added gently. "We all do it."

"And get your damned foot off that center aisle," snarled Hathaway. "What do you think you are? Special or something? If everybody else can walk around, you can too.

The door slammed and slammed again. Rawlings walked into the latrine.

"Where's Roberts? Has anybody seen Roberts? He isn't on CQ."

"KP," answered Delaney. "Remember. He got night KP for a week."

As Rawlings left and headed upstairs, Alvardo came in, kicked aside a crushed beer can, took a look at the washing machine and shouted, "Sullivan! Sullivan!"

Beaulieu answered, "He's still on CQ."

"Then fuck him. I've got to get this wash done tonight."

"Cool it, buster," said Delaney. "My bag's ahead of yours."

"Fuck. All my fatigues stink. The sweat's been fermenting on them for weeks. Sometimes I think they're more alive than I am."

"Well, don't blame it on me," said Delaney. "Mine stink just as much as yours do. It's the fucking system's fault, giving us one washer for forty-seven stinking guys."

"When I get out of here," said Beaulieu, "I'm going to write a book about this shit-hole."

Frank looked up from his notebook. "Just remember not to make a big deal about all this. It isn't like we've got it bad. After all, we're Reservists and National Guard. It isn't like we're going to be shipped to Nam. We aren't that low in hell. We all have homes and jobs or school we expect to get back to in a few months. We've got to be careful because we've got something to lose. This isn't your usual basic training."

"Yeah," Delaney added, "we've got it easy. The system has given us a few advantages, and we've taken them, so we've got a stake in the system. We don't have as much of a stake as the runts and cowards, but we can be counted on not to shout too loud, not to be too violent. That's how the system perpetuates itself — by giving us things we'd be afraid to part with. We have to be willing to lose everything, to destroy everything, if we ever hope to attain freedom.

"That's what's holding us here, you know — our little compromises with the system. There aren't any walls or armed guards — just imaginary lines. One step beyond the line from this tree to this building and you're AWOL. One step over that yellow line into the center aisle and...

"We don't worry about the drill sergeant anymore. It isn't a question of what he'd do to us. We've internalized it all. We react automatically. It's like they took out our minds and replaced them with machines. Or rather, we did it to ourselves so we could be good little boys without having to think about it. We form 'good habits,' like good little boys."

Waslewski casually crushed the last beer can, raised himself from the laundry bags, and stumbled out of the latrine toward his bunk. He nearly bumped into Alec and Evans by the water fountain.

"What the hell's this paint crap?" Alec asked Evans.

"If you've got to play the game, why not play to win?"

"God, I don't see how you can take this crap seriously."

"But I don't take it seriously. So they say, don't cross that line. What the hell should I care? Do I really need to cross that line? Hell no. If it were something important, that would be different. But this is all nonsense. So why not play along and beat them at their own game?"

"Don't you have any guts?" asked Alec. "You just buckle under and do everything they tell you. Don't you have any self-respect? Damn it, why don't you stand up for yourself sometime. Rebel."

"Rebel? What the hell for, Alec? Why the hell should you want to step over that line? Why make a big deal of it? It only takes a minute to walk around. If they're dumb enough to want to make a rule about it, okay – humor them a bit. If you see it as a game and get into the swing of it, you can have some fun, instead of just griping all the time. You sound like you want to break rules just because they are rules. Whatever anybody said not to do, you'd want to do it. There's nothing more childish."

"Whatever anybody said to do, you'd do it. There's nothing more childish," Alec mocked.

"Hell, Alec, get the old team spirit. With freshly painted lines, we'll be sure to win the Monday inspection by a wide enough margin to win for the week. That'll give us three weeks we've won and two ties. One more win after that, and we'll have clinched the barracks competition. The second platoon will probably take the PT competition. But we have a good shot at the rifle and the G3, and a damn good chance to come out best overall platoon."

"Maybe you've got a stronger stomach than me," said Alec. "Maybe you can eat more shit than I can without getting sick. Maybe you can even learn to love eating shit. But I've reached my limit. Just one bit more and I'll... I'll..."

"Gripe some more?" offered Evans.

Alec clinched his fist, glanced toward Hathaway's bunk, leaned over the water fountain, took a swallow, spit it out with a grimace, and stomped to the latrine, sliding a bit in his stocking feet.

Upstairs, Rawlings sat up in his bunk, and stretched his arms. There was too much noise in the barracks to sleep, even with the door to his and MacFarland's room shut. It seemed like they were yelling and stomping about on purpose to annoy him. He wrote a letter to Madeline:

"I know you must find it strange getting these letters from me. Sure we parted as 'friends.' I haven't forgotten. There's no way I could forget it. But you have no idea what it's like here, what hell it is. I need someone to write to, someone to dream about. Just to keep my sanity, I need it. Please let me delude myself a bit. Please don't keep hitting me over the head with a sledge-hammer. After all, how can either of us know what things will be like in three months? People change. Just let me believe there might be a chance.

"Sometimes I regret ever having gotten myself into this mess. I should have paid some dentist to put braces on my teeth and avoided the military altogether. But I always planned to go into politics after law school. I hate the Army. I know there's no moral justification for Nam. But to get elected to a position of authority so I can do something to prevent future Nams, I have to have served in the military. It's one of the unfortunate facts of politics, one of the compromises that have to be made.

"There's nobody here I can talk to, except maybe Powell. And there are very few occasions I feel free to talk to Powell.

"The rest of the platoon hates me for not standing up to the drill sergeant, for not voicing their wants and opinions. They have little direct contact with him or with the senior drill except for receiving commands. They have little notion of what those sergeants are like, how they think and react, how you have to deal with them.

"Friday night while I was sleeping, someone sprayed shaving cream in my open mouth. They've played pranks before, but that one shook me up. I might have smothered to death or gone into shock. I think it was MacFarland, the assistant platoon leader who shares this small room with me. It took so long to wake him that he must have been faking that he was asleep. It gives me a creepy feeling knowing that the guy I've been living so close to could do such a thing.

"I've been on my guard since then. So many of them have it in for me. Delaney, especially, hates me; and he makes no attempt to disguise it. I wouldn't trust Alec or Waslewski either.

"There's no way for me to find out who got me with the shaving cream. I'm sure all the others know who did it, but none of them would tell me. I knew they wouldn't and that it would be best not to say anything. If they thought they'd gotten my goat, it would encourage them to do more of the same. So I pulled myself together, told MacFarland, 'It was nothing, go back to sleep, just some practical joke.'

"Then at Saturday morning's inspection I got a gig for shaving cream on my bedpost. I hadn't noticed it. If I'd told the drill sergeant how it got there, he'd have made trouble for everybody. He's had it in for me lately. I've gotten several gigs — just little things I'd absent-mindedly overlooked, like forgetting to hang a towel at the base of the bed or not displaying a laundry bag. It's bad enough when we don't win an inspection, (he'd put anybody with a gig on night KP for a week), but when the platoon leader gets gigged, he blows his top.

"He's been riding me for not being more strict, for not asserting my authority, for not giving him the names of slackers so he can punish them. He claims there's no excuse for me getting a gig, that I should have two or three of the others make my bed, straighten my area, check and recheck. But I can't see burdening the others with my problems. They've got little enough time to do their own work.

"Anyway, the sergeant has clearly reached his limit. If anything more goes wrong, no matter how minor, there's no telling what torture he might put us all through."

———————

The screen door slammed . Sullivan shouted, "Has anybody seen Roberts?"

"Keep it down," whispered Delaney. "He's AWOL, but he might come back. If Rawlings hears about it, he'll rat on him and we'll all get screwed."

"But what if he doesn't come back? We can't cover for him forever, and it's a serious offense if they find out we've been covering for him."

"Cool it. Just cool it," whispered Delaney. Then out loud he said,

"What were you saying Beaulieu?"

"Just that somewhere there's got to be a good place to live, where you can really be yourself."

"No, don't kid yourself," explained Delaney. "It's Catch-22. The world of business and the world of the army. Milo Minderbinder runs the whole show. The army's just a big business, an equal opportunity employer — with all the bureaucracy and waste and impersonal cruelty of a big business.

"Read the papers, man. They want junior officers for management positions. The foremen are no different from old sergeants. They are sucked in by the gradual increments in pay, the pension plans, and all that crap.

"From the outside, the Army looks like a bunch of guys who shoot and get shot at. But from the inside it's padded with bureaucrats trapped in a web of slowly accruing benefits. All you've got to do to be able to cash in your chips at age 65 is cover your ass. You never have to do anything that might tax your mind or your energy. Just never make a blunder without covering up for it.

"The whole setup breeds paranoids, security-hungry paranoids spending all their time trying to divest themselves of responsibility, following the letter of the regulations and passing the papers to the next desk. It's dangerous to make a decision. Any change is dangerous because it shifts the rhythm of covering up activities. You might miss something.

"The Army's probably the most conservative institution in the world. It has carried the inherent tendencies of big business to their natural extreme. It's the epitome of business.

"If you feel crushed and oppressed here, if you feel they've torn down your world and thrown you naked and helpless into a world of their making, well, it's just a model of what goes on out there — what you're going to go back to."

———

As Rawlings was licking the envelope, he glanced down at the floor beside his bed. His boots were missing — his second pair of boots, the ones that he never wore, the ones with the special glossy shine for inspections, the ones that every morning he had to remember to dust off or he'd get a gig.

He stood up suddenly, dropped the letter on his bunk, got down on his belly and crawled under the bed. He could see nothing. He reached and reached again through empty space.

He checked MacFarland's boots. They had MacFarland's name tag.

He checked under MacFarland's bed.

He checked his own wall locker.

MacFarland's wall locker was locked.

With his strength, he'd have had no trouble breaking it open. But a bent locker, too, would be a gig.

He checked his footlocker. He knew the boots couldn't be there, but he checked under the underwear he'd never worn, so carefully rolled for inspection. He checked under the handkerchiefs he'd never used, behind the shaving cream, under the razor he'd never used, under the shaving brush that he wouldn't even know how to use.

There were no boots. MacFarland's footlocker was locked.

"Where the hell are my boots?" Rawlings bellowed. The whole barracks fell silent.

He stood at the top of the stairs as half a dozen puzzled trainees gathered below. "This has gone far enough," he announced. "I want my boots back."

Another dozen gathered to watch and listen.

"Where are they?" he repeated. His voice was getting shrill.

"Where are what?" asked Tag.

"My boots, you fool."

"On your fucking feet," said Tag. "Why didn't you leave them at the door like the rest of us?"

Everybody but Rawlings broke out laughing. Attracted by the laughter, the crowd grew larger.

Rawlings slowly and deliberately came down the stairs. "Where the hell is MacFarland?" he insisted.

"Right here, Fats," MacFarland answered, winning a few laughs.

"Well, give them to me."

"What?"

Rawlings now stood face to face with him. The rest of the platoon crowded close around.

"The boots. Give me the fucking boots!"

MacFarland stared him hard in the eye.

Rawlings started shifting his weight from foot to foot and clenching and unclenching his fists.

"Give him the boots!" shouted a voice from the front steps. "The boss wants boots."

Suddenly, a hail of boots came flying through the door at Rawlings.

One hit him hard on the side of the head. He lost his balance and fell backward. Rather than catch him or cushion his fall, the crowd moved back. His back hit the floor; his head the bottom step.

He grabbed the banister and pulled himself to a sitting position on the stairs. "Where are my boots?" he insisted.

"I bet Roberts has them," came a shout from the crowd.

"Or maybe the boots have Roberts," suggested someone else.

"Yeah," shouted the first, "I hear the boots went AWOL and took Roberts with them."

"Just where is Roberts, anyway?" Rawlings asked. He pulled himself to his feet and tried to reassert his authority. "Where is he?"

Cohen started humming the tune "Freedom's just another word for nothing left to lose."

"Yeah, man," somebody whispered. "He's free, free as a bird."

"Down with the king!" shouted drunken Vassavion. "Give me liberty, or give me MacBeth!"

"Shut up!" shouted Rawlings.

"Now is the summer of our discontent," Vassavion continued.

"I said – shut up!" Rawlings shoved him. Vassavion shoved back. Rawlings shoved Hathaway by mistake. Hathaway swung wildly. Rawlings ducked and rammed his shoulder into Hathaway's belly. Waslewski punched Rawlings in the back. Rawlings fell, swinging boots and feet wildly, tripping Vassavion, Hathaway and Waslewski. They rolled and slid down the sacred center aisle.

The whole platoon gathered around, standing and leaning on the bunks, watching the fight. They were a mob ready to erupt, to release its pent-up hate and fear and frustration on this petty platoon leader.

Delaney jumped up on a footlocker, raised high a fist, like a lightning rod and shouted :

"Power to the people!"

"Power!" repeated a dozen others.

"Power!" chanted dozens more.

"Down with all pigs!" shouted Delaney.

"Right on!" chanted the chorus.

"Kill the fucking bastard," someone mumbled.

The chorus laughed nervously.

Rawlings tried to stand, was tripped by Waslewski. Hathaway dove on top of him, pinned arms with knees, and started slapping his face back and forth, harder and harder.

"Give him one for me!" shouted someone.

"And for me."

"And me," echoed up and down the room.

"Give him one for the Gipper!" shouted Cohen. Everyone laughed, so Cohen continued, clapping his hands, "Go team, go!"

The crowd responded, "Push him back, push him back, way back."

Cohen grabbed two of the many boots lying on the floor, pulled them on untied, and started jumping and dancing like a cheerleader.

"Power!" repeated Delaney.

"Power!" repeated the chorus.

Vassavion stumbled to his feet, waving his arms drunkenly. "For mine is the power and the glory!" he yelled.

"Go get him, Vass!" shouted the crowd.

"Give him that boot he wanted," someone offered.

"Give him this one!" shouted someone else throwing a boot to him. Vassavion pulled it on his right foot, and stood, unsteadily between Rawling's spread-eagled legs, his toe near Rawling's crotch.

"Give him a Vass-ectomy," someone muttered.

Then the room was quiet, except the slap of palm against cheek, as Hathaway kept hitting mechanically and rhythmically. Everyone watched, both hoping and fearing the drunken giant with the boot would kick.

The quiet was becoming oppressive. "Hold that line! Hold that line!" Cohen chanted loudly, wanting to be the center of attention again. No one responded.

Then Cohen took three running steps and slid heels-first down the center aisle, tumbling into Waslewski, who knocked over Vassavion. He left a long ugly gash down the middle of the floor.

"The time has come!" shouted Delaney, raising his hand high. And once again attention focused on Delaney. It was like he was taking them up the steepest incline of a giant rollercoaster, and they both feared and wanted to reach the peak and race to the finish. "The time has come!" he repeated for emphasis. "Now we must..."

Suddenly he was lifted high in the air. Powell had grabbed him by the seat of the pants, and dangled him, like a rag doll, over the center aisle.

"Help!" gasped Delaney, when he finally realized what had happened.

"Enough," announced Powell, softly and firmly. Then he tossed Delaney on the floor, like throwing a bag of garbage in a dumpster.

Hathaway stood up. Schneider helped Rawlings get back on his feet.

Delaney, crouched by a footlocker, murmured, "I told you so. I told you about the system..." but quietly and cautiously.

The screen door slammed. "Half an hour till lights out!" shouted the CQ, a squad leader from second platoon. "God. What the hell happened?"

"Nothing, buddy," growled Hathaway. "Nothing at all. Just turn yourself around and get the hell out of here."

"God, looks like you had an explosion or an orgy. Somebody sabotage the place or something?"

"Get your goddamned boots off that center aisle," roared Hathaway.

"You've got to be kidding. There's nothing I could do to it that hasn't been done already. Whoever did that sure did a hell of a job. Was it the first platoon?"

Hathaway picked the stranger up by the shoulders of his fatigues.

"Okay, okay, I'm going. It wasn't me that did it. You don't have to take it out on me."

The screen door slammed behind him.

Quiet, subdued, without anyone having to give the orders, they pushed the bunks back to the walls and got on with their chores. Powell, Schneider, Tag, and three others were soon on their hands and knees rubbing a new coat of wax on the floor, while Evans carefully repainted the yellow lines.

Alec, Alvardo, and even Delaney went to work on the stairs with toothbrushes, scrubbing away at the corners and crevices. Frank and the latrine crew started to work on the johns and urinals. Alec whined, "Those damned shitheads have closed off the latrine again. One damned urinal and one damned john is all they ever leave us. Shit. When I have to shit, I have to shit."

"That's the system for you," muttered Delaney. "They have barracks inspections theoretically for the sake of hygiene. But in the Army, what matters is the looks, not the facts – just what can be neatly filled in on an official form. That latrine will be clean. It'll be spotless. But to keep it as spotless as we have to, we can only use it half the time. The rest of the time we've got to go piss under the trees.

"There's no place on the official form to indicate whether the latrine is used or not or to indicate the level of the stench out there under the trees. So we pollute the one bit of shade where we can rest for a break, and we end up sitting on our own piss.

"They told us to keep the latrine spotless. That's how the system works. We wind up seeming to do this to ourselves. And we are, after all, guilty – guilty of going along with the game, playing by their rules. And every time we do, we wind up sitting in our own piss."

"That's sounds fine, Delaney," admitted Alec. "But let's face it – we all can't be Roberts. We were born comfortable, and we want to stay comfortable. We sold our souls long ago. And cheap, too, goddamn it. Of the whole bunch of us, only Roberts is free."

Delaney just kept scrubbing. He looked weary. There was a bad bruise under his left eye. It was swelling.

MacFarland was one of the few who were just trying to look busy. He kept washing and rewashing the same clean, easily reachable windowpane. But even that was an improvement – he had never before felt obliged to act like he was working. As assistant platoon leader, he was officially exempted from such tasks. But now he kept glancing about guiltily; and when he thought someone was looking, he made a show of putting tremendous effort into the cleaning of that one clean windowpane.

Everybody but Rawlings was working. Rawlings had shut himself in his room to tend to his wound, to try to make the scratches and bruises as inconspicuous as possible. His display boots had miraculously reappeared, with a few minor scuffs, on top of his bed.

While buffing those boots, he tried to reconstruct a poem – something he had written that May in the midst of the frustration of Cambodia and Kent State. He wished he could have remembered it, could have recited it before, to have let the other guys know that he felt the same anxieties and frustrations they did, that he was with them, not with the system, that he was and wanted to be one of them.

The effort of trying to remember helped him to calm down and pull himself together, helped him to feel again that he was a college student among college students. Once again the complex and baffling world was painted in bright colors – right and wrong, good and evil. Once again, he knew what to hate and hated in unison with thousands of others.

He grabbed paper and pen and wrote from memory:
In May the bombs blossom.
The sweet aroma of gas fills the air.
The sing-song
Mekong
May song me

doe
ray
me lie me down to sleep, and pray the Lord (what else can one two
three four,
right face
the press
of the crowd,
shouting,
mad men giving orders
on the borders of insanity,
a neutral nation,
at least officially,
but everyone knows thyself
is an archaic term in jail, waiting for trial,
by hook or by crook, we'll pull this impotent giant to a hard line on
and on and on and onward,
Christian humility in defense of freedom is no situation comedy,
featuring
Nixon, Mitchell, Agnew, and a fourth horseman of the Apocalypse
to be announced,
so stay tuned to looney tunes, on most of our network stations,
brought to you by,
bye
happiness is a warm gun,
in the age of hilarious,
who cannot wash away our sins with a flood of tear
gas,
for there was a limited supply of war,
one day
in May the bombs blossom.

It was clever. Ever since he first wrote it, he was proud of how clever it was. But now it sounded false and hollow. Now that he had been at Fort Polk, had slept in the same barracks, shat in the same johns, low-crawled over the same gravelly field as men who had died in that war he wrote so cleverly about...

He felt ashamed and embarrassed. It was like he'd been behaving like a five-year-old brat, whining in a candy store because he couldn't have exactly what he wanted.

What right did he have to feel sorry for himself? Just a few more weeks of hell and he and the rest of the platoon – all but Roberts and Armstrong and those two new guys – would be going home. Who could blame Roberts for running? Chances were that in a few months he'd be in the jungle waiting for the booby trap or bullet that would turn him into rotting meat. And, by then, Rawlings would be starting law school.

He crossed himself, then went over to the window and stared out at the row of barracks and the scrub pine forest beyond.

Polishing the water fountain, Sullivan wondered what the folks back home were doing to his car. He'd bought it new, and from the very beginning there had been some crazy link between his life and its.

It was a bright red convertible. He'd bought it the summer he thought he was going to marry Diane. Whatever it was in him that urged him to buy that car knew damn well that he wasn't ready to get married. And when Diane saw it, she knew too, and it wasn't long before they went their separate ways. That car – a '53 Chevy with an exterior in mint condition – always broke down when he was supposed to go some place but really didn't want to go. At those moments, from a sense of responsibility, he would go to great lengths to try to get it running, but much to his relief, it was mechanically impossible.

There was something wrong with the electrical system. He'd gotten a new battery, a new generator, a new voltage regulator, a new solenoid – but still it would happen. He'd turn the ignition and get a feeble click.

But when he really wanted to go somewhere, without fail, the car would turn right over.

This had happened so many times that when the car failed to start, Sullivan no longer got mad. He just sat and thought about it for awhile and tried to figure out why he really didn't want to go where he was going since the car was clearly telling him he didn't.

So when he had to go to basic training, he had grave misgivings leaving that car behind. He'd grown to depend on it for his social life, as a relief from recurring restlessness, as a source of freedom, and as the physical manifestation of his inmost desires.

He couldn't help but wonder what his parents were doing with his car. It seemed almost obscene giving them control over that secret part of him. But he had had no choice but to leave it. That was one of things about basic – as Delaney said, they made you surrender body and soul, every parcel of your dignity and freedom.

Cohen started singing again, softly, till others joined in. Even Sanderson joined in.

"I got to get out of this place..."

"Oh Lord, how I want to go home..."

"Freedom's just another word for nothing left to lose..."

"On the first day of Christmas my drill sarge gave to me..."

"Fuck the army, fuck the army, fuck the army..."

"For he's a jolly good fuck-off..."

"Power to the people..."

Alvardo did some drill sergeant imitations on the staircase.

"He sounds more like a drill sergeant than the drill sergeant does," commented Beaulieu.

It was then that Sullivan took down the plaque to polish it. Looking it over, he exclaimed, "Shit! It's all here. The same damned wisecracks. They scribbled them here on the back with all their signatures. This thing must be twenty, twenty-five years old, and they were making the same dumb wisecracks we are."

Everybody knew what they had to do, and they'd all done it, quickly and efficiently, like a well-drilled team. The floor still had to be buffed, but first the wax would have to sit for awhile, and the paint would have to dry.

While waiting, Tag read his four-day-old newspaper. It appealed to his imagination that it was old. Everything could have changed in the meantime, like they were in a time warp: living in the same world as everybody else, but four days behind. The rest of the world might already be a better place.

Beaulieu lay on his bunk and wrote to Marge:

"I want to put it all down while it's still fresh in my mind, even though I don't know what it means. I just want to get it down on paper before I forget it.

"I forget so fast here. Usually, that's a God-send, but this time I want to remember, so maybe later when I look at it, when my head's rested and clear, when I'm me again, I'll be able to make sense of it, rework it into a story, maybe learn something so all this hell won't have been for nothing.

"God, we get used to it quick. Just five fucking weeks I've been here, and half the time I forget I've got a fucking uniform on. Five fucking weeks and I have a hard time imagining myself back home in civvies, going to work in the morning, sleeping with you at night. Seems like some fucking dream, doesn't it. Something far, far away.

Just five fucking weeks, and it's like I've never been anything but a fucking solider.

"Delaney was right about the system and what it does to people. But there's something else going on here, too.

"Through all this muck and shit, it had been damned good hearing Cohen cut up the drill sergeants and hearing Alvardo imitate them to a tee. We had them pegged. We knew who they were, knew how petty and mechanical and predictable their minds were. No matter what they might do to us, we had that knowledge, that feeling of superiority.

But now we see the same damn crap on a World War II plaque. Some originality. Wind up the toy soldiers and listen to the noises they make. Hell.

"Schneider, (he's been hanging around with Powell a lot), said something about there's nothing new under the sun.

"Vassavion sobered up a bit in the shower. He said something pompous about history. And he was right. All along we've been acting like this was something new, like nobody'd ever been through basic before. This was our drill sergeant, our barracks, our army, our country. But we're just here for a little while. We're just transients. There have been millions before us, and there will be millions after us, and there's nothing particularly noteworthy about us and what we've said and done. It's all been said and done before.

"Our 'revolution' was no big deal. We scuffed up the floor a bit. By the time Powell gets done with it, it'll all be good as new, almost – all but that jagged mark down the middle. He can't get rid of that. The linoleum was scratched.

"And we should be proud of that? That's what we'll leave for posterity: a jagged scratch on a piece of linoleum.

"Silly though this competition business is, it is a shame to leave a blemish like that for the next cycle of trainees. The guys that came before us did such a good job on it that we hardly had to touch that center aisle for it to come out shining unbeatable. I wonder how much work went into that, how many years of work by generations of trainees who never met each other, who knew that they would never meet each other, but who left this as a legacy to whoever might come after them — this so fragile shine that was, ridiculously, such a source of comfort and security and pride.

"Even though we had done nothing for it, or practically nothing, except refraining from messing it up, it was 'our' floor; it was 'our' barracks. We did take pride in it.

"I hope that Powell can do something. He has such a way with that buffer. If anyone can do it, he can. And I certainly do hope he can erase or at least hide it.

"We've got four weeks left. Maybe by then it'll be all right, and the next cycle will get it good as new, as good as we got it, as good as if we'd never been here and messed things up. Maybe a little better, with those yellow lines repainted.

"Yes, it looks sharp with those bright yellow lines."

The screen door slammed, "Five minutes to lights out!" shouted the CQ. "God, it looks good now. When the buffing's done, you guys could be in good shape."

"Maybe there won't be an inspection," offered Schneider, as the CQ went away.

"Yeah," whined Alec, "you can count on it: if we get the place in shape, they won't inspect it."

"And if we didn't, they would. We'll be ready," affirmed Evans. "I just hope those damned bat exterminators don't come again."

Hathaway laughed, "Have you grown to like the bats?"

"We can live with bats. I just don't want the exterminators messing the place up. We can still win tomorrow."

Long after "lights out," the barracks still hummed with the sound of the buffer and clanked with the sound of opening and closing lockers. Everybody had something that still had to be done.

The screen door closed softly. A whispered, "The drill sergeant's coming."

Those words repeated echoed and reechoed through the muffled scrambling of feet and creaking of bedsprings. Whispers followed, racing up and down both sides.

"He's going upstairs."

"It's Rawlings he's after, Rawlings. He's bawling out Rawlings."

"Now the shit's going to hit the fan."

"He probably heard..."

"No, it's Roberts."

"Roberts?"

"Shit."

"You say Rawlings is ratting on Roberts?"

"That goddamned Roberts."

"Goddamned my foot. He's the only one of us with an ounce of guts."

Footsteps echoed on the stairs again. The screen door closed again, softly.

Silence. A full minute of absolute silence.

"Roberts!" came a loud whisper from the bunk nearest the door.

"God! It's Roberts," was repeated up and down.

In the conflicting shadows of the fire light and the stair light, Roberts slowly rubbed his freshly shaved head with his towel.

"Quick, Roberts, catch the drill sergeant. Rawlings just ratted on you. You're in a heap of trouble. Catch him, and let him know you're here."

"He knows I'm here all right. What's this bit about ratting, man? What have I done that somebody's ratting on me?"

"This is the Army. You don't just go home when you feel like it."

"Home? Who the hell went home?"

"Well, where've you been?"

"Taking a shower."

"Yeah, but where've you been all night?"

"Look, man, cool it. I just got off KP."

"Well, then what was the sergeant pissed off at?"

"Me. He saw me in the shower. You know, man — no showers after lights out. But I'll be damned if I'm going to bed stinking of garbage and shit. Hell no, man."

"There's your freedom, Alec. There's your dignity."

"Yeah, damn it, I didn't have guts enough to take a shower."